Touch Me Gently

By the Author

Bareback

Long Shot

Call Me Softly

Touch Me Gently

Touch Me Gently

by

D. Jackson Leigh

2012

TOUCH ME GENTLY

ISBN 10: 1-60282-667-6
ISBN 13: 978-1-60282-667-0

This Trade Paperback Original Is Published By
Bold Strokes Books, Inc.
P.O. Box 249
Valley Falls, NY 12185

First Edition: June 2012

THIS IS A WORK OF FICTION. NAMES, CHARACTERS, PLACES, AND INCIDENTS ARE THE PRODUCT OF THE AUTHOR'S IMAGINATION OR ARE USED FICTITIOUSLY. ANY RESEMBLANCE TO ACTUAL PERSONS, LIVING OR DEAD, BUSINESS ESTABLISHMENTS, EVENTS, OR LOCALES IS ENTIRELY COINCIDENTAL.

Credits
Editor: Shelley Thrasher
Production Design: Susan Ramundo
Cover Design By Sheri (graphicartist2020@hotmail.com)

Acknowledgments

This story is for my buddy, Phoebe, who insisted that insurance agents can be sexy, too.

A special thanks also goes to my beta readers: Jenny, Gail, and Debbie. You guys are primo.

Also, I have to give a nod to the amazing Bold Strokes Books staff, authors, publisher Len Barot, and my most excellent editor, Shelley Thrasher. They are truly like a second family.

Last, but not least, I will always be grateful to Angie for shoving me down this road to being an author.

Dedication

For Lacey J, the best damn Jack Russell terrier ever. Her brave little heart touched mine every day of our sixteen years and five months together.

CHAPTER ONE

Salem Lacey was frozen.

She couldn't move her feet to run. She couldn't move her mouth to speak. Every extreme emotion she'd ever experienced was an ice pick poised to pierce the indecision that encased her.

She wanted to laugh hysterically at the absurd scene before her. She wanted to scream her rage at the betrayal. And she wanted to sob at the fixed, unseeing stare on her dead lover's face.

State Representative Eve Sutherland's gardener lay naked, spread-eagle on her belly with her wrists and ankles securely tied by silk scarves to the four posts of the queen-sized bed. Eve sprawled on top of her, her bare buttocks framed by the harness of a strap-on dildo still buried between the gardener's legs. Eve's head was turned to the side, her eyes and mouth open as though she was permanently surprised.

"Get her off and untie me." The gardener groaned. "Please, my arms hurt."

"Shut up so we can think," Salem's friend, Alisha, snapped.

Numb, Salem barely felt Alisha's arm curl around her shoulders. This didn't make sense. Nothing had made sense from the moment Alisha woke her at six o'clock and demanded that she come to Eve's house immediately.

The owner of an exclusive housekeeping business, Alisha visited each location to make notes of things that required special attention or reallocate workers to the messiest houses. She started very early with the homes of friends who didn't mind when she let herself in to inspect while they were getting ready for work.

"I'm so sorry, hon. I shouldn't have called you. The house was so quiet, I thought Eve must have stayed with you last night. So when I opened the door and saw this, I panicked." Alisha spoke gently. "I've phoned Jeffrey. He'll know what to do."

"Jeffrey?"

Eve was in the middle of a fiercely contested re-election battle and Jeffrey was her campaign manager. He was deeply closeted, just like Eve and most of their high-powered friends, and would know how to cover this up.

"I should have let him take care of this and told you about it later."

How could Alisha be so calm?

"Please," the gardener whined. "Get her off me."

"We've got to do something," Salem said, but she didn't know what.

Less than twenty-four hours before, Eve was making love, and promises, to her. They'd returned to Atlanta around eight o'clock last night after spending a romantic weekend in the North Georgia mountains. Eve dropped her off before going to her own house, explaining that she had a fund-raising breakfast to attend very early the next day and needed to prepare a brief speech.

"Alisha?" Jeffrey's voice floated up from the downstairs foyer.

"Up here."

He pounded up the stairs. "I don't care what the problem is, she's scheduled to be at a critical fund-raiser at seven thirty. If she's drunk, we have to sober her up fast. If she's sick, I've got Craig on standby to shoot her up with one of his super drugs that'll get her through the morning." He stepped into the bedroom and stared. "Eve—"

Alisha scowled. "She can't hear you, idiot. I think she's been…gone…for a while."

Jeffrey stared at Eve. "Holy fucking shit. She's dead?" He pulled his phone from his jacket and tapped in a number. Jeffrey was a rising star among campaign managers because he was cold-blooded and clear-headed in even the worst crisis. Eve used to joke that he'd infect a baby with pandemic flu if he thought he could get the opposing candidate to kiss it.

"Get her off me." The gardener was starting to hyperventilate and Salem felt like she might join her.

Jeffrey walked to the end of the bed, the phone pressed to his ear, and peered at the bodies. "Is that thing still stuck in there? Damn, that's gonna hurt. Craig, I need you at Eve's house right away. You don't have time for coffee. This is big, very big. Reschedule your morning appointments, but don't tell anyone where you're going."

The gardener struggled against the tightly knotted scarves. "Untie me. Get her off me, please. Oh, God, get her off me."

Her pleading rubbed against Salem's exposed nerves like sandpaper. She closed her eyes and gritted her teeth. "Do something."

"I am doing something," Jeffrey snapped. "Craig's house is just a block away. God damn it. You'd think she could keep it in her pants for another few months, just until I could get her re-elected."

The gardener began to sob. "It hurts."

Jeffrey knelt next to the bed. "Calm down and listen to me. It'll hurt a lot worse when we untie you and pull that dildo out. A doctor's on the way. He'll give you something—"

"Christ almighty!" Craig shoved past her like the stocky rugby player he was and threw his physician's bag down next to the bed. "Lesbians and their toys. Those things ought to have a warning on the box. You can't fall asleep like that. The vaginal tissues dry out and they wake up stuck together like dogs." He glared at Jeffrey. "Why can't you have a normal emergency, like somebody's arm stuck in a wood chipper?"

Jeffrey, tall and a little too slender for a man, stood and firmly grasped his boyfriend's jaw. He forced Craig to meet his gaze. "Listen to me. I need you to be calm. We need to be very careful how we handle this. They're stuck like this because our friend Eve is dead."

"Get her off me." The woman's sobs were growing weaker.

Craig looked down at Eve when Jeffrey released his grip. "Son of a bitch." He probed her throat for a pulse and ran his hand down her arm. "Rigor is starting, so we need to hurry before she gets too stiff."

"What are you going to do?" Salem swayed. Her paralysis was wearing off, but she felt helplessly weak.

Jeffrey grasped her elbow and turned her toward the door. "Craig and I'll handle this. You need to go home, sweetie."

Alisha frowned. "What *are* you going to do?"

"Fix it to look like she died in bed alone before we call the police. That's all y'all need to know. You two were never here." He waved for Alisha to leave with her. "You should follow her home and stay with her a while to make sure she's okay." His words spoke of compassion, but his eyes spoke his real message. *Make sure she keeps quiet.*

"Fine with me. I don't want anything to do with this." Alisha grabbed her hand, but Salem turned back to the bed.

Gazing at Eve's face one last time, she realized the woman who had been her lover was gone forever. So were four years of memories, because she would remember only this when she thought of Eve. It was a cold blade through her heart.

"Eve…how could you?"

Chapter Two

Knox Bolander leaned against the door of her black Jeep Wrangler and watched the small crowd gathered to pay their last respects. Even with a football field of distance between the group of mourners and where she'd parked under the gnarled oak, she felt the chill of the open grave as though she stood next to it. When they lowered the bronze casket into the Georgia red clay, a piece of her would stay with it.

She'd seen little of her father, Robert Hamilton Bolander, over the past twenty years. Though not an openly affectionate man, he'd been a kind and steady presence in her life. She'd stopped coming home after her brother died, so her father visited her in Maryland once a year. He gifted her with two of his most prized Friesian mares, and they spent the day riding before going out to dinner and perhaps the symphony. The visits were short, only a day or two, and her mother never came with him.

She treasured those times and suspected that their trail rides provided his only respite from the melancholy that had enveloped him since the dreadful day that changed all of their lives.

They'd lost much more than the eight horses who perished in the fire that gutted the Bolander stable. Her mother retreated back into therapy, Knox was packed off to the Institute, and her twin brother Ham was pulled from public school and secluded at home for the rest of his life.

Robert Bolander had carried the heavy burden to his death, and Knox could never purge the nightmarish fire from her memory.

She could still feel its heat and hear her father's shouts and the frantic neighing of the trapped horses as she dragged her hysterical brother to safety. She could smell the acrid odor of her own singed hair and clothing.

The turmoil of her bitter thoughts made the branches of the moss-draped oak she stood under begin to stir. The leaves fluttered even though the sweltering summer day was windless, and the old priest standing at the head of her father's casket paused to stare. He crossed himself and mouthed a prayer of intercession. Knox's mother, a tall woman dressed in ambivalent gray, never looked up. But others at the gravesite followed the priest's gaze and joined his prayer.

She hadn't experienced such a lapse in many years. Shaken, she ordered her thoughts and clamped down on her emotions. The branches stilled, and she climbed into her Jeep and drove away.

❖

Knox reined her horse to a walk and turned onto a wide sandy path that wound under a canopy of oaks and pines common to the Georgia lowland. After leaving the cemetery, she had driven to the Bolander estate to saddle the youngest of the three horses her father still kept. She followed the circuitous route among the pastures and cultivated fields they had often ridden together when she was young.

The Bolander estate had once covered 1,500 acres near the Georgia-Florida border, where her great-grandfather originally raised cattle and farmed cotton, peanuts, and corn. Later, he added a shaded tobacco operation that elevated the Bolanders from mere farmers to one of the region's wealthiest families. He had planted more than a hundred acres of tobacco under the shelter of thousands of yards of loosely woven cheesecloth to grow fine, unblemished leaves that became the "wrappers" for cigars. When regular tobacco sold for forty cents a pound, her family got four dollars a pound for the shaded tobacco.

But growing shaded tobacco was labor intensive and the market peaked in the 1960s, then waned as labor costs soared. So the family tore down the hundred or so aging houses where farm workers once lived and sold much of the land to developers for millions. The Bolanders quit farming and leased their remaining 500 acres of fields to other farmers so they could spend their time tending their money instead.

The afternoon ride gave Knox a chance to sort through the new changes in her life, and when she stopped her horse at the destroyed stable, she found it strangely appropriate that her route ended where her journey had begun.

She dismounted and stood among the weeds and briars that threatened to cover the stone foundation left intact when the burned rubble of the Bolander stable was removed.

The gentle Friesians they bred were dark and sleek with a smooth, high-stepping trot. She and her brother were only four years old when her father had placed Ham, then Knox in the saddle in front of him. Her brother had cried to get down, but Knox was thrilled and Robert had even let her hold the reins for a short time.

The next day, he began her formal riding lessons. Fearless, she refused the pony he wanted her to try. So he lifted her into the saddle of a placid Friesian mare, where she perched like a tiny jockey as she guided her horse to follow his. Their rides together had begun.

A multi-millionaire by birth, Robert Bolander was a historian and philosopher by choice. It might have seemed odd to discuss the history of civilization with a child, but Knox wasn't a normal little girl. Her very advanced brain absorbed every word as they rode the maze of paths on their property. She loved her father and those lessons...almost as much as she loved her twin brother.

"Don't cry, Knox-Knox."

"She took him to the pound this morning, Ham."

"Who, Knox? Who did Mama take?"

"The dog I found. His leg was hurt. I wanted to call Doc Evan. He could have fixed him."

"How did he get hurt? Did he fall down? Daddy put a Superman bandage on my knee when I fell down and it's all better now."

"I wanted to keep him, but she wouldn't let me."

"Daddy'll be home tomorrow. We'll go get him. Daddy can put a bandage on his leg and make him all better."

She whirled around and petals exploded everywhere, leaving a ravaged bed of headless tulips in her mother's prized garden.

"Oh, no! You did it again. Mama's going to be really mad." They were only eight years old, but Ham was big for his age. He wrapped her in a tight hug.

"It's too late," she cried. "I called. They put him to sleep because he was hurt."

Uprooted foliage flew through the air around them.

"You gotta stop, Knox. We can wake him up. We'll tell Daddy tomorrow when he gets home and he'll tell them to wake him up."

"He's not sleeping, Ham. That's just what they call it. They killed him. She took him and they killed him. She's so mean. I hate her. She hates me."

"I love you, Knox-Knox. Don't cry."

She let the tears trickle down her cheeks unchecked, as if brushing them away would erase the memory of her brother. Knox and Hamilton's chiseled good looks were their only similarity. Athletic, she also possessed a stunning intellect that made her a whispered name in the math and physics world by the time she was fifteen. Ham, born mentally handicapped, had a weak heart that gave out two days after his eighteenth birthday. She was his Knox-Knox, and he held her when she skinned her knees or had a bad dream, because her mother wouldn't, couldn't.

Someone was approaching, but she didn't turn until her horse raised its head and nickered to the newcomer.

"Hello, Knox."

"Hello, Mother."

"My camellias and gardenias are thriving this year."

Claudia Bolander, a classic beauty, had the same gray eyes and dark hair as Knox. While not on the genius level with her daughter, she possessed a sharp mind and artistic flair. Claudia also suffered from Asperger's syndrome, a form of autism. Years of medication, careful therapy, and an environment constructed to cater to the peculiarities of her handicap allowed Claudia to enjoy her understanding husband and become a locally acclaimed artist. But she lacked the empathy and emotions to be a nurturing mother.

Knox wasn't surprised that Claudia acted as though it had been days, rather than ten years since they'd last seen or spoken with each other. She wasn't upset that her mother didn't seem to notice the tears that wet Knox's cheeks. She understood that while the remark seemed out of place, Claudia was actually attempting to reconnect with her.

The estate's gardens obsessed Claudia, and, as a child, Knox spent hours helping plant, weed, and prune the flowers in an effort to have some kind of relationship with her.

"I saw them. They're beautiful," she said.

Claudia twisted her hands together and shifted from foot to foot. Knox always found her mother's elegant features a strange contrast to her graceless, sometimes clumsy movements, reminiscent of Ham's. Was that why she always forgave her mother's shortcomings?

"You have to take care of them for me. I won't be here to do it," Claudia said.

"Are you going on a trip?" Her mother rarely traveled. Leaving her familiar environment or changing her established routine stressed her.

"I'm going to Florida to live with my sister."

"You're leaving for good?"

Claudia began to pace. "I can't stay here. Things aren't right, not right at all." She spoke a little too loudly as her anxiety mounted. "There's a hole where he was. The house, the garden…they're different without Robert. Not right at all. You'll take care of them, won't you? You'll look after my flowers."

"Yes, of course I will. I'll take care of everything."

"But you don't live here. They need care every day. The weeds will grow, the blossoms will die. They'll die without someone to look after them."

"I can move back, Mother. I've been thinking of it anyway."

Claudia stopped pacing. "Good. That's good, then. It's all yours now…the house, the gardens, his horses. I don't want any of it without Robert here."

"When are you leaving? Do you need help with the arrangements?"

"No. Christine's here. Didn't you see her at the funeral?"

"No. I wasn't there long." Knox had been eight years old when she last saw her aunt, so she doubted she'd even recognize her. Christine would be the best person to care for Claudia, though. A psychiatrist inspired by her sister's disease, she'd built a practice that specialized in autism.

"You must behave while she's here, Knox."

Knox frowned. It wouldn't do any good to explain that she had learned to control her emotions and her special ability years ago, because she hadn't exactly demonstrated that skill earlier at the cemetery. "I'll be careful."

"We're leaving in the morning. Driving to Florida. I can't get on an airplane. Airplanes crash, fall from the sky. Chris says they grow orange trees in Florida. She has lots of flowers that need tending."

"I'm sure you'll be very happy there."

Claudia began to pace again. "They have hurricanes in Florida. I'm a little worried about hurricanes."

"Not where Aunt Chris lives. I'll bet some maps will show they don't usually hit that part of the state. You could look them up on the Internet."

"Yes. I can research it."

Without another word, Claudia tramped stiffly through the weeds, back to the manicured lawn and expansive house. That didn't surprise Knox either. Her mother was simply unaware that she should say something to excuse herself from their conversation. And if Christine didn't prompt her, Claudia might leave for Florida in the morning without saying good-bye, not realizing they might never see each other again.

Knox turned back to the scorched stones. They were still a solid foundation.

She couldn't reconstruct her lost childhood, but she could rebuild the stable. Everyone was gone, but she was coming home.

Chapter Three

"Get ready." The cameraman held up his hand and silently counted down the seconds until they were on the air. When he pointed to the reporter, she began her spiel.

"Hundreds of mourners are filling the Atlanta First United Methodist Church today to say good-bye to State Representative Eve Sutherland, found dead in her home on Monday. A preliminary coroner's report blames an undiagnosed heart defect for the premature death of the most promising young politician this state has seen in years. Although she was currently campaigning for a second term in the Georgia legislature, rumors have been circulating for months that her party would tap her to run for Congress when Senator Ed Talmadge retires in two years."

Salem hesitated, then walked quickly past the television crew. Eve had never mentioned running for Congress, but she had apparently forgotten to mention a lot of things.

Salem understood the political reasons, but was never happy that the woman she'd loved for the past four years had been deeply closeted. Eve insisted that they live in separate houses and always had some dashing young male lawyer escort her to public events.

But she had grown tired of being invisible in Eve's life.

So, on Saturday she had taken a chance and given Eve a very expensive diamond necklace—a ring would have been too obvious—and proposed that they spend the rest of their lives together. They didn't have to go public right away, Salem explained, but she wanted them to at least take the first step and live in the same house.

Eve accepted the necklace and vowed they would talk about moving in together right after the election. Her assurances of love felt more like a campaign promise than evidence of a commitment, but Salem tried to ignore that as they spent the rest of the weekend in bed, stoking the fires of passion.

"You holding up okay, hon?"

Salem held on to Alisha's hug for a long moment. Despite her Ivy League education, highly successful company, and exclusive clients, Alisha was the most real of Salem's friends. She never forgot her roots as the daughter of a maid and what it was like to grow up in the Atlanta projects.

"I don't know, 'Lish. I still feel numb, you know. Like I'm going to wake up from a really bad dream." She blinked to clear the tears blurring her vision. "I had no idea she was seeing anyone else."

Alisha tucked Salem's arm in hers and guided them up the walkway toward the church. "Sweetie, I can't pretend to understand how Eve's brain worked, but you were the only one who meant anything to her. All the others were just impulses she couldn't seem to control."

Salem stiffened. "All the others? There were others?"

"Well, shit. I put my big foot in that, didn't I?"

"You knew she was cheating on me and never told me?" A pinhole of light suddenly penetrated the darkness that had been drowning her since Monday morning. "Did anybody else know Eve was cheating on me?"

"Girl, we all knew. We thought you did, too."

Anger rose in a hot flush to burn her cheeks. She rounded on Alisha. "How many others?"

Alisha tugged her into the church. "I have no idea."

"Venture a guess, just for me? Two? Three? One a month? One a week? Did she fuck other women several times a day while I stupidly thought we had an exclusive relationship?"

"Keep your voice down." Alisha pushed her along a short hallway and into the ladies' restroom. "I don't know. You think she kept a list or that I followed her around to count?"

Damn it. Salem paced the small room. Lying, disloyal slut that she was, Eve had cheated her one last time by dying and stealing from her the pleasure of slapping her face. She balled up her fist and thumped Alisha hard on the shoulder instead.

"Ow!"

"Why in the world would you think Eve cared anything for me if she was fucking every bimbo she hired to chauffeur her or cut her grass or clean her house?"

"Oh, no. She never touched my employees. I personally told every one of them they'd be jobless the instant I found out she'd been in their panties."

"Well, I guess that's something."

"I'm not the enemy, Salem. Have any of our other friends called or come by to see how you were doing?"

She stared at the floor and didn't answer.

"I didn't think so. They're paranoid that one of Eve's bimbos will out her for some tabloid cash, then them by association."

She drew a deep breath and exhaled loudly. Alisha was right. She cast about for at least one good memory of Eve and their relationship. "Why did you say I was the only one she cared about?"

"Because you were her Plan B, girl. I overheard her and Jeffrey talking. If she ever got outed, they decided she wouldn't risk denying it and getting caught in a lie. She planned to stay a step ahead of the media by going all Ellen on them and announcing her engagement to you. She was going to ask you to marry her."

"I was to be her trophy wife." How calculating could you get?

"I hadn't thought of it that way." Alisha put her hands on Salem's shoulders and waited until their gazes met and held. "Let's just get through this funeral, then I'll take you wherever you want, to do anything you want…even get drunk in a strip bar. But first, I have to pee and you have to fix your makeup."

While Alisha disappeared into a toilet stall, Salem studied her bloodshot eyes in the mirror, then dug into her purse for eye drops and mascara. She combed her fingers through her hair. It was time to freshen the highlights in her shoulder-length dark blond locks.

She was applying a liberal coat of lipstick to replace what she'd managed to chew off when two women burst into the room and crowded up to share the two-sink vanity and mirror with her.

"That man is an idiot if he thinks I'm going to stand out in that heat to smoke my cigarette. I'll bet you can fry an egg on the sidewalk." The woman eyed her seventies-era hairstyle and pulled a long cigarette from her huge purse. She bumped Salem's arm, causing her to smear lipstick across her cheek. "Sorry," she said without a trace of sincerity. She lit the cigarette and watched her reflection as she blew smoke through her nose, then mimicked the usher in a snotty tone. "I'm sorry, ma'am. You can't smoke in this building."

Salem dampened a paper towel to scrub her cheek, but made room at the sink while Alisha washed her hands.

"I'll wait for you outside," Alisha murmured, indicating the overcrowded room.

The second woman ran a comb through her long dark hair. She looked to be around thirty, but her eyes were hard like someone who had seen many more years. "Give me a drag off that before you put it out," she ordered the smoker. Something about her and the bracelet on her arm seemed familiar to Salem.

"Lord, Laine, I coulda died when I saw that big house of hers," the smoker said, handing over her cigarette. "And you and Aunt Verna living in that old doublewide. She ought to be ashamed."

"Evelyn always was a selfish bitch. Dear old sis ain't been home for a visit since she left for that fancy-smancy college up north. She did pay off the mortgage on Mama's trailer and sent a few hundred dollars every month, but we didn't have a clue she was some big-time politician right here in our home state. Her letters always had an Alabama postmark. She didn't want us to know where she really lived. I'll bet she sent us less than what she paid her maid every week."

Laine? Elaine? Eve had once mentioned a sister named Elaine. But when Salem probed for more information, Eve simply said she'd divorced her redneck family and never looked back once she escaped the Georgia swamps and went to college. She usually told people she didn't have any surviving family. Salem stared at Laine's reflection in the mirror. She could see the resemblance now, around the eyes and chin.

"We would have never knowed she was living here if Buddy hadn't been driving a load up to Charlotte and seen it on TV at a truck stop." Laine applied additional blue eye shadow to her already heavily painted eyelids.

"You being family, we should have stayed at her house."

"We would have if that fruitcake hadn't shown up and thrown us out. At least he paid for our motel rooms at the Days Inn. Pretty fancy, huh?"

"Not as fancy as Evelyn's house. So, who gets that house and all her stuff? Evelyn wasn't married, was she?"

"No, she weren't married, but we don't know if she left a will. At least I got a look in her jewelry box before the fruitcake showed up and ordered us out. Wish I'd had time to go through her closet, though."

"You wouldn't have gotten in the house at all if I hadn't picked the lock on the back door," Laine's friend reminded her. "I didn't get nothin' for my trouble."

Laine looked thoughtfully at the bangle bracelet on her wrist, then slid if off her arm and handed it over. "You can have this. I got her diamond bracelet in my bag. It goes better with this necklace anyway."

"Hey, thanks."

Laine fished around in her purse and pulled out a diamond tennis bracelet. She held it up to her chest next to the diamond necklace she wore.

The diamond necklace.

"That's my necklace." The two women stared at Salem.

"Who are you?" Laine narrowed her eyes.

"Salem. Eve and I were…close. I just gave her that necklace last weekend."

"Then I guess it ain't yours anymore," Laine said.

"She promised me something for it, and I never got it because… of what happened. So I would like to have the necklace back, please."

"I think you're mistaken that this is the same necklace."

"I had it custom made. There's not another like it." The pendant consisted of two gold hearts entwined. Inside one heart was a diamond-encrusted *S*. In the other, an *E*. "It has our initials on it. You had no right to take it."

Eve's sister narrowed her eyes. "Still queer, was she?" She laughed. "Well, it works just fine for me and my boyfriend, Sam. You snooze, you lose," Laine said, dismissing her and turning toward the door. "Let's go find a good seat for the show," she said to her friend.

Salem stepped in front of the door. "I want that necklace."

She never saw it coming, but the slap was hard enough to rattle her teeth and slam her head against the door. The women pushed her out of the way and left before she could respond.

❖

"Shit, girl. What happened to you?" Alisha stared at the handprint on Salem's cheek. "I leave you in the bathroom for five minutes and you get into a cat fight? This isn't junior high, you know."

Salem couldn't stop the tears of frustration. She was so angry, yet so helpless to do anything about it. She choked out the story of the necklace, beginning with her proposal to Eve and ending with Laine's slap.

"Aw, honey. Go ahead and cry. Nobody expects your makeup to be perfect at a funeral." Alisha wrapped an arm around her shoulder and offered a small packet of tissues she pulled from the pocket of her blazer. "This will be all over soon."

They crowded into a pew filled with people Salem didn't know. Eve's political cohorts, no doubt, drawn by the chance to step in front of the local television cameras filming from the balcony and every corner of the room.

She didn't know what Jeffrey had promised Eve's sister and her friend, but they sat quietly tucked away in the balcony. When she spotted them, Laine was watching her. Her blood boiled when Laine smirked and fingered the diamond pendant.

Jeffrey had tightly choreographed the service, so they had to sit through at least an hour of political eulogizing before he pulled out his ace card.

He was tall, dark-haired, and handsome, one of Eve's preferred escorts, a hanger-on with political ambitions. What was his name? Jason? No. It started with an M. Mike? Merlin? Mackey?

He stepped up to the pulpit, wiped at a non-existent tear, and cleared his throat.

"I'm Mason Whitaker. I fell in love with Eve when we were in law school, studying together over cold pizza and diet soda." He stared down at the pulpit as though collecting his emotions, then cleared his throat again. "But Eve had greater things in mind than marrying right out of school and starting a family. She asked me to give her time, and I had to respect that." He paused to blink rapidly and hang his head again for a moment. He took a dramatic deep breath.

"Careful, buddy. Your overacting is a bit obvious," Alisha muttered.

"What the hell is he talking about?" Salem whispered loudly. She recalled Eve laughing about how dumb Mason was, thinking his looks would be enough to get him elected. He was a minnow stupidly wanting to swim with sharks, she said.

"Politics is a chess board of compromise, trading off small things to win the big prizes. But Eve had conviction and loyalty. She refused to concede even the small things that didn't fit with her high standards."

Oh yeah. That's why she lived a false life, stuffed away in the closet crowded with lies of love and all the women she was fucking. This guy was really pissing Salem off.

"We need that kind of leadership in our great state, so I occupied myself building my law practice and waiting while Eve laid the foundation of her political career. I can't express how much I regret being too busy to find time for more of our special dates."

He played out another dramatic pause.

"They didn't date." Indignant, she forgot to whisper and several people seated around them frowned at her.

Mason continued his eulogy.

"The doctors say she died of an undiagnosed heart defect. But I think Eve sensed something was wrong. We spent last weekend at a romantic cabin in the mountains, talking about our ambitions and what we wanted in life. She said, 'Mason, if anything should ever happen to me, I want you to run for my seat and finish what I've started.' 'That's ridiculous,' I told her. 'Nothing's going to happen to you.' She begged me to promise, so I took a chance and said I would if she'd marry me. She said yes."

"Liar!" Salem sprang from her seat.

She was through compromising because she loved Eve. It had been small things at first: pretending to be just a friend, dragging along Rob and Jeffrey on ski weekends to keep up appearances that they were two heterosexual couples. But somewhere along the way, the lies chipped away at her self-worth. She had come so close to selling her soul she was disgusted with herself, furious with Eve, and irate that Jeffrey had trotted out this moron and was setting him up to take Eve's place in her campaign.

"Eve was at that cabin with *me* last weekend. That's right. Eve Sutherland was a lesbian. We've been lovers for the past four years. It would have been a little hard for her to be making plans with this idiot while she was naked in bed with me all weekend."

She whirled toward the balcony and pointed up at Laine.

"And that's my necklace that hick is wearing. She stole it out of Eve's jewelry box."

CHAPTER FOUR

Knox pushed her cart along the aisles of the Piggly Wiggly grocery, staring at the colorful array of boxes and cans. She'd never had to shop for food before. A meal service had kept her freezer stocked with gourmet dinner entrees she could heat in the microwave. When she remembered to eat lunch, it was usually a salad or sandwich from the Institute's employee cafeteria. She wasn't much for snacking, and the only junk food she'd ever eaten was pizza when the guys in the computer lab ordered it and included her.

She stared at the bags of potato chips. How was a person supposed to know which one to buy? She took one from the shelf and read the list of ingredients. Did people really eat this stuff? She put the chips back. Maybe she could survive on the rotisserie chicken, sandwich fixings, fresh fruit, and bag of pre-packaged salad in her cart.

When she rounded the corner, three women and their carts stood mid-aisle, whispering together. They glanced nervously at her and stopped talking. She pretended to study the ingredients on a box of cereal. Although two of the carts were pointed in her direction, the women turned them and hurriedly escaped.

Knox sighed. Even after all these years, the gossip about her still thrived.

"Look at you, all grown up and gorgeous."

Knox turned at the familiar gravelly voice and smiled for the first time in what felt like forever. "Doc Evan. Hey."

Crow's feet and smile lines creased his tanned face, and gray streaked Dr. Evan Shepherd's dark hair now, but the eyes that twinkled under his bushy eyebrows were just as she remembered. It was twenty years ago, but felt like yesterday that she was eight years old and trailing after him to ask a million questions as he vetted her father's horses.

"I thought that was you at the cemetery, and when I saw a Jeep with Maryland plates in the parking lot, I took a chance I'd find you in here. If you're grocery shopping, you must be planning to stay more than a few days."

"Actually, I'm not doing much shopping." She shrugged. "I don't know how to cook and don't have a clue what to buy."

"Someone taking care of you up there then? Someone special?"

"A food service kept my kitchen stocked with precooked meals."

He looked disappointed. "I can't believe, with your looks, a crowd of young men isn't trying to get in your front door."

Knox frowned. "My house is in a gated community. They'd have to have permission to get past the guard."

Doc shook his head. "You need to look up from your computer once in a while, girl."

She folded her arms over her chest. "I'm not oblivious. Just not interested."

"Don't get your dander up. You always were touchy and I'm just being a meddling old pest." He glanced down the aisle at a woman who had pushed her cart near them and appeared to be reading every word printed on a box of sugary cereal. "You didn't answer my question. You planning to hang around town a while? I'm guessing you're here to do something about your father's horses. I know Claudia isn't interested in keeping them."

"Actually, I'm making arrangements to move back. Mother left yesterday to live in Florida with her sister. I plan to rebuild the stables and send for my two horses."

Doc turned toward the woman reading the cereal box. "Did you get that, Margaret? Knox is here to stay. Claudia's moved to Florida. You can stop pretending to read that box without your glasses.

You've got your gossip, and I'm sure the rest of the hens are dying to find out what you've overheard."

The woman huffed at him and hurried away to find her friends.

He turned back to Knox and clasped her shoulder. "That's wonderful, honey, just wonderful. I sorely miss your dad, but you're a sight prettier than he was."

Knox stared at the floor, forcing herself not to flinch. It was rare that anyone touched her. Her unique ability and her intellect had always separated her from everyone else. But this was Doc Evan, she told herself. He'd never treated her as anything other than a normal little girl.

"They've been following me since I came into the store." She shifted her feet. "Maybe it was a mistake to think I could come home."

Doc grasped her chin and forced her eyes up to his. "It was not a mistake. For every one of those gossiping old biddies, there're two others like me, who're happy to have you back here. Don't you forget that."

Knox doubted anyone but Doc Evan and her mother were glad she was moving home, but she didn't want to talk about it any more and shrugged it off.

"All right then. Let's find you something to eat that you don't have to cook. I'm an expert at that since Janie passed a few years back."

"I'm sorry. I didn't know." After losing the only two people she was close to, she knew how lonely he must feel.

He waved off her sympathy. "'S okay. It was cancer. She was in so much pain, we were both ready for her to go when it happened. I've had some time to get used to it." His gruff tone was dismissive, but his eyes said he still missed his wife. He commandeered Knox's cart and headed toward the frozen-food section. "Let's get you some groceries, young lady. Then you can join me for lunch at the diner."

Wednesday's blue-plate special was fried chicken, mashed potatoes, and black-eyed peas. It'd been days since Knox had a hot meal and she dug into the food with gusto.

"Tell me what you've been doing up there in the big city," Doc said as he salted his food without tasting it. When Knox hesitated, he put the saltshaker down and lowered his voice. "It's not classified, is it?"

Knox shook her head. "I just don't want to bore you to death."

"It can't be more boring than my usual lunch conversation with Harley about how to cure his hogs' intestinal parasites or with Earl about his prostate troubles."

She grimaced. She didn't need that image in her mind while she was eating lunch.

He chuckled. "I feel the same way. So, anything you have to say has got to be better."

"I write computer programs for virtual-reality simulators."

"You mean like the things they use to train pilots?"

She nodded. "I've done a few of those, one for the military. But since I finished medical school, I've been working on programs for virtual triage, diagnosis, and surgery."

"How does that work?"

She explained one program she'd written that allowed medical students to practice heart-valve replacement on a virtual patient.

Doc sat back and scratched his chin. "Amazing."

"Can I get y'all anything else?" The waitress refilled their glasses with iced tea sweet enough to plunge a healthy person into a diabetic coma. She looked to be in her late thirties, with friendly eyes and a long blond braid that hung down her back. "Maybe a couple more pieces of chicken?" Knox was caught with her mouth full, but nodded an affirmative.

"Bring us some more drumsticks, if you please, Gina," Doc said.

The diner had been hopping when they first arrived and Gina had little time to do more than seat them in a back booth, get their order, and serve them. But the crowd had thinned now and all her customers were munching on their meals. So, after she set a plate with one drumstick next to Doc and another with three next to Knox, she propped a hand on one hip and openly checked Knox out.

"I'd hoped that one day you'd improve your lunch company, but I've got to admit you've done a whole lot better than I would've given you credit for."

Doc frowned at the division of drumsticks, but made the appropriate introductions. "This is Knox Bolander, Robert's daughter. Knox, this is Gina."

Caught with her mouth full again, Knox smiled.

Gina cocked her head and smiled back. "Well, well, well. So this is the famous Knox Bolander. That's funny. You don't look like the devil incarnate. But then the preacher always said the devil comes in many attractive disguises."

"Gina—" Doc's scowl held a stern warning.

Knox swallowed and wiped her mouth with her napkin, her taste for fried chicken gone. "No, it's okay, Doc Evan. I'm done here."

She threw some money on the table and started to slide out of the booth, but Gina shifted to block her from standing up. "Now don't go gettin' all upset. I wasn't saying nothin' about you. I was poking fun at the gossips that came in here for pie and coffee after your daddy's funeral. Here, let me take that empty plate."

Knox shot Doc a look, but he was gnawing on his chicken leg, apparently deciding to let the two of them sort this out. So she sat back while Gina gathered the dishes.

"You haven't even eaten your pie, hon. If you don't like apple, we've got homemade pecan. Would you rather have that? Maybe with some vanilla ice cream on top and coffee to go with it?"

Knox nodded. "Yeah. Thanks."

"Not any of that decaf stuff," Doc said.

Gina returned quickly with two mugs of coffee, a slice of pecan pie à la mode, and a takeout box filled with drumsticks. "The pie's on the house, sugar. I'm sorry if you took my teasing wrong. Last week, those gossips were saying my baby sister, Maxine, was the devil incarnate. She's the good-looking butch at Johnny's garage. Max has fixed every one of their cars and 'serviced' more than half those hypocritical bitches, if you get my drift."

Doc spewed coffee onto the remains of his pie and coughed into his napkin until his face was red.

"It's true," Gina said, helpfully pounding his back. "Anyway, I'm just saying that Knox here is this week's gossip. They'll be on to something else next week."

"Um, thanks, I think." Her earlier irritation eased, she had a hard time not liking Gina's open, affable personality.

Gina beamed at her. "Well, I'll let y'all finish up. You don't be a stranger now. Tomorrow's special is meatloaf and peach cobbler. Mae's peach cobbler isn't something to miss."

Knox stared as Gina headed over to a table full of men holding up their coffee cups to signal they needed a refill.

"I swear. I never know what's going to come out of that woman's mouth," Doc said. "She's good people, though."

They sipped their coffee and Knox shoved the last of her pie into her mouth. She chewed thoughtfully before she spoke in a low voice.

"I don't do it any more, you know."

The doubt she read in Doc Evan's expression reminded her that he, too, had witnessed her visit to the cemetery.

"That was just a slip," she said. "I've learned to control it so it doesn't happen…hasn't happened in years. I told them I must have grown out of it, that I can't do it anymore."

Doc shook his head and spoke softly so no one would overhear. "I was wondering how you managed to get away from that Institute to move back here. You must be the only person in the world who can do what you do."

Knox shrugged and pushed the crumbs of her pie around with her fork. She wasn't at liberty to tell him there was a handful of others. It was a highly classified government secret.

"What you have is a gift, Knox. You shouldn't have to hide it."

He was wrong about that. As a child, she didn't know how to focus her ability, which only surfaced when her emotions peaked. It scared normal people and fascinated the scientists at the Institute.

"God only knows what else that brain of yours could do if you tried. You could accomplish a lot of good in the world, girl."

"I'm doing that now, Doc Evan, in the computer lab. One of the programs I'm working on will let a cardiac doctor in a lab at Johns

Hopkins actually operate on a patient on the other side of the world via satellite, using virtual technology and surgical robotics. And I'm privately working on a program that will eliminate the need for those animal labs everybody hates by providing virtual humans for drug testing." She sat back and sighed. "I don't want to be different anymore. I just want to work at my computer and ride my horses."

Doc pursed his lips thoughtfully, then nodded. "You do what you have to, honey, and to hell with anybody who tells you different." His expression was sympathetic. "You've already carried a burden no child should have to bear. That stupid fire stole your childhood and your father's soul. I'll always believe the guilt led to his early death. He could never forgive himself for letting the gossips pin the blame on you."

"I didn't come back to dispute those rumors, Doc. I don't care what they say about me. Swear you won't say anything. Swear to it."

His eyes were sad. "Your father took that secret to his grave. I'll do the same if that's what you want, but I wish you'd reconsider. Nobody's left for you to protect, Knox. It happened twenty years ago when you were a minor. They can't possibly charge you with insurance fraud."

"Mr. Lacey knew. He could be charged with conspiracy for letting a false claim go through."

"Franklin Lacey is dead, too. He died about a month ago."

CHAPTER FIVE

Salem drove her red BMW slowly up the short driveway to the modest brick home with a roof pitched steep for design rather than function, since it never snowed in South Georgia. Neat beds of azaleas lined the foundation on either side of the three steps leading to an arched front door. She continued under a drive-through carport on the side of the house and parked her car just short of the freestanding garage in the backyard.

The trip from Atlanta had been more than four hundred miles through endless small towns and speed traps to reach the most southwestern corner of the state where her father, Franklin Lacey, had lived for the past seventeen years. She was exhausted and desperately wanted to shower after a painfully full bladder forced her to take care of business in one of the nastiest gas-station restrooms she'd ever imagined. She should have just pulled off the side of the road and used the woods. Even a case of poison ivy on the tush would be preferable to what she might have been exposed to in that gas station.

She got out of the car and stretched before fishing the house keys from her pocket and trying them in the back door. The lock turned easily and the door swung open to reveal June Cleaver's kitchen. The cheery yellow room had ruffled curtains in the windows. The sink, cabinets, and appliances lined two walls, and a 1950s-style Formica-topped table sat in the center of the room. The appliances were old, but well maintained. Even better, the smell of oatmeal-raisin cookies permeated the air and caused Salem's stomach to growl.

She picked up a note someone had left on the table. Cookies were in the oven, the note said, and hopefully still warm, depending on what time she arrived. Fresh bread and cereal were in the pantry, milk, sandwich makings, and a pitcher of sweet tea in the fridge if she was hungry. It was signed, "Welcome to your new home, Lucille."

Who the hell was Lucille and how did she have a key to the house? Maybe it was the wife or secretary of the lawyer who had been executor of her father's will. Didn't really matter. Salem was starving and too tired to go out and forage for food. At least she felt like eating. It had been weeks since she'd had an appetite.

She nibbled a cookie and hummed with pleasure before cramming the rest into her mouth. She was reaching for another when a loud meow nearly made her jump out of her skin. A scrawny kitten was climbing up the screen door and yowling up a storm at the smell of food.

"Don't feed strays or you'll never get rid of them," her mother had always said.

So she went outside and pulled him down. "Let go, ya little bugger. I'm not going to feed you." She walked to the edge of the yard and set him there. "Go back to wherever you came from. Don't make me take you to the pound. That's where they put little kittens in the gas chamber."

She hurried back to her car, grabbed her luggage, and sprinted into the house, closing the door solidly behind her to keep the tantalizing food smells in and the dirty little stray out.

The décor of the living room was more masculine than the kitchen. No ruffled curtains in here. But the leather sofa and recliner looked fairly new, the small fireplace had been updated with gas logs, and a fifty-four-inch flat-screen television dominated one wall. Her dad had still been the football fan she remembered. College and NFL memorabilia hung on the walls and sat in various places around the room.

The house had only two bedrooms, and one had been converted into an office. She was pleased to see the bathroom off the hallway had been updated, but the master bedroom was the real surprise.

On the bedside table sat a picture of her in her Emory University cap and gown. A family photograph taken in the North Georgia mountains sat on the massive cherry dresser. She was about ten years old and held onto a canoe paddle as she stood in front of her parents. Her dad's arm was draped over her mother's shoulders. Mom was laughing, while Dad and Salem wore huge grins.

At the center of the dresser was a misshapen ashtray filled with coins. She had made it in the third grade and given it to her father. Finally, there was a framed picture of her parents' wedding day with Mom and Dad staring lovingly into each other's eyes.

She frowned.

It was a shrine to the family he had wanted them to be, she decided. The loving, adoring wife and the obligatory child to prove he was man enough to reproduce.

❖

Franklin Lacey had been a conservative Republican insurance salesman and a devout Southern Baptist. Sylvia Devereaux was a liberal Democrat and a free spirit. She also was the director and choreographer of an Atlanta dance troupe.

Salem always thought their differences had attracted them to each other. He was drawn to her mother's wildness and she to his stability. They were a happy family.

Franklin went to church on Sunday mornings while Sylvia slept late. Saturday-night performances usually kept her at the theater into the wee hours, and she often had a Sunday-afternoon matinee.

Salem went to church with her father as a small child, but her mother made sure she was exposed to other religions and permitted to make her own choice when she reached her teens.

By then, her friend Amy had pointed out that Southern Baptists believed women weren't capable of having a leadership role over men and should be submissive to their husbands. That didn't sit well because Salem held a very low regard for boys, whom she found generally stupid and juvenile. The ones who did seem to have a brain were just geeky.

So she rejected her father's church and joined her mother's routine of sleeping in on Sunday mornings. Unhappy, Franklin urged her to at least investigate other Protestant denominations and even offered to go with her to visit some churches. He would keep an open mind if she would, he said.

But Salem's mind was opening to much more interesting things, namely Kath O'Malley, captain of the girl's basketball team. She could stare into Kath's blue eyes all day. They went to summer camp together, and Salem took ice hockey rather than figure-skating lessons because Kath did.

They shared everything—their lunches at school, music, sports, and even clothes. Well, shirts and jackets. Kath had grown unusually tall for her age so they couldn't share jeans. They were like Siamese twins from the time they were twelve until they were fifteen and discovered they also liked to share kisses.

It was the beginning of Salem's discovery that she was attracted to women.

It was the end of her happy family.

They hadn't done anything but kiss, but they were heavily into it when Dad had knocked quickly on the bedroom door and stuck his head in to see if they wanted to go for ice cream.

He went ballistic.

Mom was at work, so they were at his mercy. He called Kath's parents and ratted her out when they came to pick her up. Salem locked herself in her room and cried for hours.

When her mother came home, her parents had a huge fight. Franklin ranted that Sylvia's lack of religious conviction had poisoned their daughter. Sylvia accused Franklin of damaging Salem's adolescent psyche by condemning her sexual exploration.

Franklin slammed out of the house, and Sylvia tried to call Kath's parents and apologize for her husband's behavior. But the O'Malleys were Catholic, and they informed her that Kath would be attending a new school on Monday morning, a school where the nuns could correct Salem's misguided influence on their daughter.

Salem would never see Kath again. Mom held her as she sobbed and whispered promises that when things seem darkest, a dawn always follows.

That dawn didn't come.

Sylvia slept in Salem's room every night that week, holding and consoling her in her dark hours. She was Salem's advocate, trying to reason with Franklin. At the same time, she begged Salem to understand that adults make mistakes, too, and her father would eventually realize his error and be very sorry for what he'd done.

But Sylvia misjudged Franklin's convictions.

On Saturday morning, he had roused them both to have breakfast at their favorite pancake restaurant.

"See?" Mom had said. "He's going to apologize, and I want you to try to understand that he loves you and forgive him."

But after they had breakfast, Franklin shared his news, which went way beyond anything they had ever imagined.

He announced that he had resigned his job and used their joint savings to buy an insurance business in the small South Georgia town where he grew up. He was moving his little family to a "healthier" environment.

Sylvia didn't say a word. She took Salem's hand and they went to sit in the car until he paid the bill and came out to drive them home.

"You'll see that it's for the best," he told them. "You can open a dance studio and teach classes," he said to Sylvia.

When they arrived home, Sylvia told Franklin he had two hours to get his clothes and get out. If he didn't, she'd be on the phone to the police. More than half of the money in their savings account came from her inheritance and the other from both their paychecks. He had no right to spend it without her permission.

He could go to the Georgia swamps if he wanted, but neither she nor Salem would be going with him.

That was the last time Salem saw her father.

Later that night, she found her mother holding their wedding picture to her chest and quietly crying. Sometimes love just wasn't enough, Mom told her.

Sylvia never remarried.

❖

Salem pushed away her memories and wondered what Franklin had told his friends in Oakboro about her and her mother.

Did he know she had grown up to have her mother's liberal views and kind heart, but his knack for business? He must have known that she, for some irrational reason, had followed him into the insurance business. Why else would he have left his business to her?

Despite her feelings toward him, Salem and her mother both wept when they were notified he had died on the operating table while having a heart-valve replacement.

Sylvia had cried again when Salem sold her house and stored her furniture to leave Atlanta, but she didn't try to stop her. Perhaps seeing where her dad grew up would help her understand him better and feel less rejected, her mom had said.

Maybe if she'd understood a lot of things, she wouldn't have impulsively outed her lover on local television. That poor decision had got her fired and sent her so-called friends running for cover. Well, everybody but Alisha.

Damn it, she didn't want to be here, but she didn't really have a choice. Hopefully she'd find his business in good enough shape to sell so she could start fresh somewhere else. She couldn't go back to Atlanta, but maybe to a city on the West Coast.

CHAPTER SIX

"Oh, my Lord, you're even prettier than your pictures."

Salem blinked. And blinked again. The only things bigger than the petite woman's teased-up hair were her oversized breasts.

First impressions are everything in the business world. What was her father thinking when he hired a red-haired Dolly Parton to sit at the front desk? Although an introduction appeared unnecessary, Salem intended to make it clear she expected a professional atmosphere in her newly acquired business. She stuck out her hand.

"I'm Salem Lacey."

The woman hesitated as she came around her desk, keen hazel eyes evaluating her. Instead of the hug Salem feared, two small, very soft…uh, very strong…hands clasped hers.

"Of course, you are. Salem's such a pretty name. I'm June Hartford, your secretary, and I'm so sorry about your daddy, sweetie. He was well loved in this town."

"Thank you." Salem didn't want to talk about her father. Her feelings about him were all mixed up, fond childhood memories battling with the bitterness of his rejection of her sexual orientation, then the surprise of her inheritance.

June gave Salem's hand a squeeze before she released it. "I understand you got into town just yesterday afternoon. The office isn't going anywhere. It'll still be here if you want to take a few days to get settled in."

"I'd rather get right to work. If you'll just show me his office, I need to go through his files and get a feel for the business."

June accepted her stiff answer without blinking an eye. "Then let me give you the nickel tour. You can leave your briefcase here until we come back inside."

Salem raised an eyebrow, but June ignored it and led her back out to the front of the building where they turned to face it.

The single-story, old-style building was common in small Southern towns. Thick, square columns held up a six-foot-deep, wrap-around porch, and large double doors opened to a wide hallway that ran down the center of the building and ended with French doors that led to a small courtyard and parking area at the back. The "dogtrot" floor plan had been remodeled to house Lacey Insurance on one side of the hallway and an accountant's offices on the other.

"The building is old, but solid. I'm telling you this because you own it. You lease the other side to another business. If their toilet stops up or their air conditioner quits, they'll call you. Of course, your daddy left that to me to handle. I don't mind it, so if you want to continue that way, just let me know. I've kinda gotten used to the kickback I get from the AC man."

Salem narrowed her eyes and June laughed, grabbing her hand and squeezing it again. "I'm joking. So serious, just like your daddy. You need to lighten up a little, honey."

Salem just nodded. She wanted to get a feel for things before she started making changes. One of the first things she would stop, however, was June's use of endearments when speaking to her and the familiar way she touched her, invading her personal space. It wasn't very professional.

They went back inside and she took a moment to appreciate the office's décor as she retrieved her briefcase. Gleaming white baseboards and elaborate crown molding framed the rich colors of the painted plaster walls. The oak flooring in the hallway was beautiful, but Salem was glad for the loose-weave Berber carpet that cut down on noise in the office.

June smiled when she noticed her scanning the room.

"My niece is an interior decorator in Savannah. When she graduated from college and started up her own business, Franklin hired her to remodel these offices so she'd have something to show off to prospective clients. That was fifteen years ago. She has several designers working under her now to keep up with all the business she gets, but she updates this office personally every three or four years."

That was one expense Salem could eliminate. She certainly could pick out fresh paint colors when needed.

They headed down a narrow hallway and June waved her hand toward an office on the right.

"That's Lamar's office. It's such a mess, I can't stand to look at it. I offered to organize everything for him, but he won't let me touch his files." Before she closed the open door, Salem glimpsed a desk and cabinets piled high with a tangle of papers and files.

"Is he out at an appointment?"

"More like out at the golf course. That's where he claims he does his best business. Lamar mostly handles commercial accounts. Franklin preferred working with personal insurance like vehicle, life, homeowner, and mortgage policies. Your daddy was a sweet, sweet man, but I always thought he needed to pay better attention to what Lamar was doing. I told him as much. 'Don't worry about it,' he said." June gave Salem a pointed look. "I think somebody should worry about it, though."

Salem nodded absently. Her mind was already past what June was saying and taking in the huge office that was her father's. Her office now. The hunter-green walls and dark-leather furniture were a bit masculine for her taste, but the beautiful cherry desk and credenza were definite keepers. She wouldn't worry about redecorating just yet. If she decided to unload the business rather than run it, she might end up selling to a man who would like the room's masculine tone. She put her briefcase next to the desk and turned to the file cabinets.

"I guess I'll get started with some of these files so I can pull together an overview of what the office handles."

June picked up a folder from the desk and handed it to her. "I've already prepared you an overview. It tells how many and what types of policies we maintain and which insurers we represent, along with a sheet of primary contacts. This second one holds financial statements for the past five years and quarterly summaries for the past two. Just let me know if you'd like to see any individual files. I'll be happy to pull them for you."

Surprised, Salem flipped through the pages. A quick glance told her this woman was more than big hair and breasts. "Thank you, that's very efficient."

June turned to go back to the front office, but paused at the doorway.

"Franklin wasn't one to tell other people's business. But in a weak moment, he did say once that you had some trust issues, and he felt responsible for that."

Salem frowned. "I haven't seen or talked to my father since I was fifteen. I don't know how he could know anything about what kind of person I am."

"I'm not getting in your business, hon. I just want you to know I'm one of the good guys. You can't go through life without somebody watching your back, and you can trust me to do just that. But you'll figure that out yourself soon enough." June didn't wait for a response. "You'll find a fresh pot of coffee in the kitchen and a mug with your name on it. Creamer's in the fridge," she called over her shoulder as she headed back to the front office.

Salem had barely sat down with her coffee, poured into a mug that literally had her name embossed on it in gold letters, and opened the first folder when the phone on the desk buzzed.

"Yes?"

"I'm sorry, hon, to bother you with calls when you're just getting settled in, but I've got Knox Bolander on line one. Her daddy died recently, too, and she's taking over his assets. She wants to meet with you, I'm sure to talk about his insurance policies."

"I'll take the call. Can you get his information for me?"

"I figured she'd be calling soon enough, so I already pulled it. It's in your inbox."

"Thanks."

She punched the button to switch lines. "Ms. Bolander? This is Salem Lacey. How can I help you?"

She wasn't prepared for the low, silky voice that filled her ear.

"I need to talk with someone about updating the insurance policies on my residence."

"I'd be happy to do that. I apologize, but I haven't had time to review your file. If you'd like to make an appointment, I'll be better prepared to talk with you then."

"Actually, I think I need to have totally new policies written. I'm building a new stable and converting a portion of the residence to house a business venture. Could we meet here so I can show you?"

Salem brightened at the prospect of writing a commercial policy from scratch, her specialty and much more interesting than insuring cars and single-family homes. She felt on solid, familiar ground for the first time since she'd walked into that awful scene in Eve's bedroom.

"As a matter of fact, I can be there within the hour if that's convenient."

"That'd be great. If you've got a pen handy, I'll give you directions."

"No need. I have your father's address. My car has a GPS."

"Well…"

"I'm looking forward to meeting you. See you soon."

Salem took a few minutes to review the Bolander file. She whistled to herself. The current policy insured a huge house and several outbuildings that included a modest barn. Ms. Bolander had said she was adding a new stable and a commercial business to the property.

And the Bolander estate was just one account. The financial statements showed a healthy six-figure income, but there was no telling how much money she could make if she could write more commercial policies in addition to the personal policies her father leaned toward. She hadn't realized how lucrative a small-town insurance office could be. Maybe she should reconsider selling the business. That is, if she could tolerate living here. She could spend weekends in New Orleans and Tampa. That wouldn't be so bad.

She threw the file into her briefcase and headed out through the front office.

"I'm going to the Bolander place. I'm not sure how long I'll be, June."

"It's out past the old cotton mill. If you wait a sec, I'll write down some directions for you."

Salem was sure "turn left at the brown cow and then right at the old Johnson place" wouldn't be helpful since she didn't know any of the local landmarks. Surely these people must have heard of a GPS. Even Walmart sold them, for God's sake.

"Don't need directions, thanks. I've got the address and a GPS."

June opened her mouth to say something, but closed it again. She grabbed one of the office business cards and wrote something on the back before handing it to Salem.

"The office number's on the front. My cell number's on the back because I'll be going out to lunch in about an hour. Call me if you get lost."

"I won't get lost. My GPS can get me anywhere."

Chapter Seven

"Where in God's name am I?"

The blacktop road Salem had turned down became gravel, then something like a dirt path a few miles back. Now, the dirt path disappeared into the black water of a Georgia swamp several feet from the front tires of her BMW.

Maybe some type of magnetic force around here was freaking out her GPS.

She surveyed the gnarled trees and a web of thorny undergrowth that surrounded her on both sides. There wasn't anywhere to turn her car around. Fine. She'd just have to back all the way out. She shifted into reverse, hit the gas, then grimaced at the sound of her tires spinning in mud. Shit.

No worries. She punched the GPS button. After several years of paying for their monthly service, she'd finally get to use this part of it.

"How can we help you, Ms. Lacey?" The male voice was friendly and confident.

"My car is stuck in mud and I need a tow truck to pull it out."

"No problem, Ms. Lacey. One moment while I locate your position and call a tow for you."

The minutes that ticked by seemed like hours. Finally, the voice returned. This time, the guy didn't sound so confident.

"I'm sorry to keep you waiting, Ms. Lacey, but we're having trouble determining your location. Our satellite shows you in the middle of a swamp."

"I think I am on the edge of a swamp, but your GPS led me here."

"There must be some malfunction. We don't show any roads leading to your current location. We've switched to visual, but the woods are so dense we can't spot your car or see any road leading to where our tracker says you're located."

"Great. So what am I supposed to do?"

"We'll contact the local law-enforcement agency to see if they can help us figure out where you are. That may take ten to twenty minutes, so you might want to switch your car off to save your gasoline and battery. It doesn't have to be running for us to find you. Please stand by."

Great. Salem sighed. Surprised she still had a signal on her cell phone, she dialed the number on the file.

"Hello?"

Damn, that woman's voice gave her shivers. She mentally chastised herself. Hadn't she learned anything from the whole Eve and stepping-out-of-the-closet fiasco? No women. She'd probably get tarred and feathered around here if it leaked out that she was a lesbian.

"Ms. Bolander? This is Salem Lacey. I hope it's not a problem, but I'll be a little later than I originally told you. If you need to reschedule, I can do that."

There was a long silence.

"Is there a problem about insuring my property?"

"No! Absolutely not." What an odd response. Why would she think that? "It's just, well, my GPS seems to be malfunctioning and I got lost. Then I got stuck in the mud and I'm waiting for BMW Assist to figure out where I am so they can send a tow truck to pull me out. I don't know how long I'll be."

"Oh."

During another long silence, Salem could hear the clicking of someone typing. "Do you need to reschedule?"

"No. I'm free for the rest of the day." More clicking. "You said your car is stuck. Are you on a dirt road?"

"Um, yes. It was paved, then it was more like gravel, then dirt. I hit a couple of dead ends, and I think I got turned around when I tried to backtrack. The road I'm on now goes right into a swamp or pond or something."

More clicking.

"Ah. I'm sure someone will be there soon. If it's all right with you, I'll be happy to meet whenever you can get here today. I don't want to proceed with the stable construction without some advice on several things that could affect my insurance rates."

"If you don't mind the delay, I'll be there as soon as they get me out of the mud."

"Good. I'll see you later, then."

Salem ended the call, thinking over the strange conversation, then glanced at the time on her phone. She wasn't good at waiting and it was hot without the air conditioner. She'd just have to roll down the windows and risk getting malaria from whatever swamp mosquitoes were lurking about. She turned the key in the ignition so she could roll the windows down, and the nav system powered on.

"Satellite signal has been lost," the robotic female voice recited. "Temporary loss of signal can result from certain weather conditions, geographic impediments such as tunnels, or atmospheric anomalies such as sunspots."

"Shit, shit, shit!"

She thought about calling June, but that wouldn't help if she couldn't tell her where she was. She turned the car off and climbed out. She'd have to retrace her tire tracks to the paved road and find some landmark or someone to tell her where she was. It couldn't be more than a mile.

Forty-five sweltering, sweaty minutes later, she finally saw a house through the woods. Yes! She hurried up to the porch and her heart sank. It obviously had been empty for some time, even though fresh beer cans littered the yard and porch. Even worse, she didn't remember driving past it earlier. Not only was she truly lost, but also separated from her car. Even if the satellite kicked back in, they would find her car but not her.

She sat on the filthy steps of the house and pulled off her heels to massage her aching feet. She felt like crying. Coming to Oakboro was a mistake. She didn't belong here. She'd traded one closet for another, and this one had mosquitoes the size of hummingbirds. When she got out of this mess, she'd find out what she needed to do to sell the business. Ha. *If* she got out of this mess.

It was only about one o'clock, but what if nobody found her before dark? Would she wander too close to the swamp and end up gator bait?

Oh, my God. What was that noise? Footsteps? She glimpsed something through the trees, moving along the road. Definitely bigger than a human. Could it be a bear?

She stood and turned toward the house. The front windows were missing, so hiding inside wouldn't help. Maybe she could find an interior room to lock herself in. She turned back to the road, fully expecting to see a bear licking its lips and running straight toward her.

Then she heaved a sigh of relief.

A large black horse high-stepped across the clearing, a tall, dark-haired woman astride him. If she'd been wearing a black cape and mask instead of faded jeans and a polo shirt, Salem would have thought she was trapped in a Zorro movie.

They stared at each other.

"Ms. Lacey?"

"Ye-yes." This beautiful woman knew her? That voice sounded familiar.

The woman pulled a cell phone from her pocket. "I found her. The old Roberts house where the high-school kids hang out to drink beer. Yeah."

She slid the phone into her pocket and shifted in the saddle. The horse neatly sidestepped closer to the porch where Salem stood, mesmerized by the woman's unusual silver-gray eyes.

"I…thought you were a bear." Crap. Being lost and sweating like a field hand was pathetic enough, but she also sounded like a city moron.

Her rescuer stared, but didn't comment. God. Was this woman just going to sit there while Salem babbled every stupid thing that came to mind? She took a deep breath and tried again.

"I was praying they would send out the cavalry, but I didn't mean it literally. Now I really feel like a damsel in distress. If you were wearing a cape and a mask, I'd swear the heat was making me hallucinate." Her attempt at a joke came out sounding sarcastic.

The woman blushed and Salem realized she was shy, not aloof. So she smiled and softened her tone.

"Is someone coming to get me or do I get to ride out of here on your handsome horse with you?"

"Max is on the way. She found your car."

As if on cue, Salem heard a truck shift gears as it turned down the path leading to the old house and pulled into the yard. A striking young butch jumped down from the driver's seat and grinned up at them.

"I'll leave you in Max's hands," the woman said, turning her horse away from the porch.

"Wait."

The woman stopped and turned back to Salem.

"I don't know who to write the thank-you note to."

That drew a shy smile.

"Knox Bolander, Ms. Lacey," she said in that husky Demi Moore voice. "Max will show you to the house after she pulls your car free. I'll have something cool for you to drink when you arrive."

With that, she wheeled the horse around and was gone.

"Yep, this is one sweet ride," Max said. "I don't get much chance to work on these babies. Cadillacs and Mercedes are the choice of the Country Club set down here." She pulled a lever to lower a fork-like apparatus and slide it under the back of the car. "But the Beemer, that's a fine piece of German machinery." She secured the car to the tow truck and pulled another lever to raise the back wheels from the mud. "I'll tow her out to the paved road where you'll have room to turn her around. You can ride in the truck with me."

Salem gingerly climbed into the tall truck, surprised to find it remarkably neat and clean. Max cranked up the air conditioner and offered her a box of moist sanitary wipes.

"Run a couple of those over your skin and you'll feel a lot fresher after being in that heat. Johnny says they make me smell like a girly-girl. I tell him that I don't care 'cause the mosquitoes hate that smell and I hate mosquitoes."

While Ms. Bolander had been a woman of few words, Max was a chatterbox.

Salem swiped the tissue-thin wipe over her face and neck. It did feel good. She shrugged out of her suit jacket to wipe down every inch of skin her silk camisole didn't cover.

"Anyway, when a pretty customer comes by and an unexpected opportunity presents itself, I don't want to be caught smelling like a sharecropper."

Salem looked up in time to catch Max quickly shift her gaze to the road in front of them. She smiled when Max's ears turned a bright red at being caught ogling.

The young woman was tall and lean, with the ropy muscles of a basketball player. Her short, spiked, dark hair and angular features were an attractive combination, but she couldn't be older than twenty or twenty-one. Even if Salem had been interested, that was too young for a thirty-two-year-old insurance agent and a sure way to rev up the town gossips. She slipped her jacket back on and Max resumed her chatter.

"I know you felt really lost, but you actually weren't far from where you were goin' in the first place. You just turned one road too soon. This is all Bolander land. It's a regular maze of dirt roads. They used 'em to move farm machinery around, but the Bolanders don't farm any more. The old man liked to ride those fancy horses up and down these trails. But then he started having heart trouble. He passed on a couple months back, 'bout the time your daddy did."

Max was a wealth of information.

"His daughter, the one on the horse just now, hasn't lived here in a long time. There're lots of stories about why, but her parents sent her away to school when she was just a kid. Dr. Shepherd says she's some kind of genius or something. Now that the old man's gone, she's come back to stay. There're a million more rumors about why she's back. I figure that's her business."

They came to a stop and Salem handed Max a twenty-dollar bill. "I have Triple A, so they'll pick up the rest of the towing fee."

After the tow truck freed her car, she pulled another twenty from her pocket. "This is for you, for being so sweet and driving out in the middle of nowhere to find me."

Max grinned. "I'd rather you let me take you to dinner sometime."

Salem tucked the twenty into Max's pocket. "You're very charming, but you'll have to settle for the twenty." She'd only been here two days and wasn't about to jump out of the closet in this small town.

"If you won't let me tune you up, at least let me get my hands on that car next time she needs servicing."

Salem laughed at Max's boldness. "I'm not sure I'm sticking around long, but if I do, she's all yours."

She was climbing into her car when Max pointed down the road and yelled after her. "First road on the left goes up to the Bolander house."

Chapter Eight

Knox paced nervously.

They could sit on the veranda, but Ms. Lacey had probably already had enough of the heat today. The air-conditioned library was a better choice.

She looked around the room, her eyes settling on the tray holding two tall glasses and a pitcher of lemonade. She'd considered offering a glass of wine or a cold beer, but alcohol wasn't advisable for someone who'd already been out in the heat too long. What if she wanted sweet tea instead? Knox knew how to put a tea bag in a cup of hot water, but she had no idea how many tea bags and how much sugar were required for a full pitcher. She should have checked the Internet to find out. She wished she had some little sandwiches or fancy cookies like her mother used to put on a silver tray when rare visitors came to call.

She needed to get a grip on herself. She wasn't a pubescent teen.

Those years had been confusing and stressful for Knox. Her newly awakened libido and mood swings made shielding and maintaining control especially hard. She was relieved when she realized that her biology leaned toward an attraction to women. In her field, her colleagues were almost always men, whose presence had no effect on her. That was helpful, but the Institute also hired a Zen master, who taught her how to refocus her thoughts and dampen her more volatile emotions. Knox became so good at it, she hadn't had to consciously clamp down on her thoughts in years.

That was, until she found Salem Lacey standing on the porch of that dilapidated house. Knox wasn't comfortable touching people, but she immediately wanted to stroke the hair that draped along Salem's shoulders like spun silk. And when those startling green eyes turned on her, they stirred something inside her. Knox could barely carry on a conversation with the woman because she was frantically throwing up mental shields. God, she probably came off like a tongue-tied dork.

She sat on the leather couch, closed her eyes, and began the breathing exercises that allowed her to center herself and calm the roiling sea of her emotions. Twenty minutes later, when the soft feminine voice of the house security system alerted her that a vehicle was approaching, she was sufficiently calm and collected.

❖

The massive three-story house made Salem feel like she'd driven from the Zorro movie set right into *Gone with the Wind*. She'd barely climbed out of her muddy car when Knox opened the front door and stepped out.

"Hello, again, Ms. Bolander." Salem juggled her briefcase and car keys, but before she could extend her hand in greeting, Knox stepped to the side and gestured.

"Please come in. We can sit in the library while you recover from your adventure."

"Thank you. It was more of an ordeal than an adventure. I really could use that cold drink you promised earlier."

That drew another small smile from her host, and Salem wondered briefly what it would be like to see a full-out grin light up her beautiful face. She mentally scolded herself. This is a business meeting, not a date.

She sank gratefully onto the plush, butter-soft leather sofa while Knox sat on the edge of a matching chair across from her. She looked pensive, as though searching for a start to their conversation. Salem waited. After all, Knox had requested the appointment.

"I hope the mud didn't damage your car," she finally said in that husky voice. She began pouring two tall glasses of what Salem judged to be lemonade from the fruit suspended among the ice cubes.

"It seems to be fine, but I'll take it to the garage later and have Max check it out. She seems competent."

Knox stopped her pouring for a minute and frowned. Salem watched as something unreadable flickered across her face, and those silver-gray eyes turned the color of dark storm clouds.

"Yes, according to rumor a lot of her customers find her very… capable."

Salem chuckled. Having spent at least five years in a closeted environment, her gaydar was finely tuned and pinging insistently over Knox Bolander. The insinuation about Max was the first step in the dance of innuendo to feel each other out. "She did offer 'special' attention, but I made it clear only my car was in need of servicing."

Knox looked both relieved and uncomfortable. Bingo. One check in the "she speaks lesbian" column.

"I don't really know her. Her sister works at the diner and recommended her." Knox's throat and cheeks flushed slightly, her gaze shifting nervously around the room.

Was she trying to let Salem know she hadn't been one of Max's customers? The subject definitely had made Knox uneasy, so Salem decided to give her a break.

"Anyway, I felt like I was lost in the swamp for hours. I'm embarrassed that I apparently was only minutes from your house the entire time. Thank you for finding and rescuing me."

Knox set a glass in front of Salem and left the other on the tray.

"It wasn't hard. I've been away for a number of years, but the property hasn't changed much since my great-grandfather farmed it."

"How did you know I was on your property?"

"You said you had satellite GPS, so I hacked into it. It may have looked like swamp to them, but I could tell exactly where you were."

"Good Lord, I had no idea it was that easy to break in to. If you could do it that quickly, what would stop some stalker from tracking me?"

"I wouldn't worry about it. That company has a very good firewall to protect its clients."

"It didn't take you long to get past it. Do you work for BMW?" Salem narrowed her eyes in an exaggerated expression of suspicion. "Or are you some kind of secret government operative?"

Knox laughed, finally appearing to relax. "Hardly. More like a super computer geek."

Salem took a big gulp of her lemonade and nearly choked as she tried to swallow. The tartness of the lemons made her mouth and throat pucker. She fell into a fit of coughing and Knox sprang to her feet.

"Are you okay? Did you swallow wrong?"

Salem struggled to clear her throat. Her voice came out in a wheeze.

"I just…it's a little…I was expecting…something sweeter."

"Sweeter?" Knox grabbed her glass and took a cautious mouthful, then made a comical face. "Holy shit. Was I supposed to put sugar in it?" She looked horrified at her blunder, but grinned sheepishly when Salem chuckled.

Her instincts were right on the money again. Knox was gorgeous when she let a genuine smile light up her features. "I'd think a computer geek would know how to Google a recipe for how to make lemonade."

"God, I'm sorry, Ms. Lacey." Knox shook her head. "Let me get you something else. I have soda, milk, beer, wine, or bottled water."

"Bottled water would be wonderful. And I'd be more comfortable if you called me Salem."

"Salem." Knox said it as if savoring it on her tongue. "Okay, if you'll call me Knox."

Did the woman have any idea how sexy she sounded?

Knox stood. "I'll be right back."

Salem watched her leave the room. Damn. It should be criminal to have an ass that sexy in jeans. It was hard to judge her age, but she didn't think they were far apart. While Knox moved with the physical grace and confidence of a woman, her tentative demeanor made her seem very young. Except for her eyes, which held the wariness of someone much older.

Knox returned with two bottles of water and set both of them in front of Salem. She immediately downed most of one, then pulled a pen and legal pad from her briefcase while Knox settled into her chair again and sipped from a soda she'd opened for herself.

"Let's get started. Are the house and surrounding properties listed in your name?"

"Yes. My father died a few months ago and my mother moved to Florida to live with my aunt. She signed all the property over to me. I have no living siblings."

When Salem looked up from her writing, she saw a flash of sadness and wondered if Knox was aware how clearly her emotions showed on her face.

"I'm sorry about your father." She tapped her pen against the notepad, trying to decide how much she needed to reveal. "I've just acquired my father's house and business here in Oakboro, but I haven't decided if I'll stay. That won't, however, keep me from writing a very good plan for you now that would continue even if I sell the business. I have a lot of experience writing commercial policies."

"That's good, then."

Salem finished the first bottle of water and opened the second. "You said you were planning to establish a business other than agriculture here. Will you have an office in this house or in some other building on the property?"

"Upstairs. I can show you."

Knox led her to a wide stairway that curved upward from the foyer. "There's an elevator, but I don't know when it was inspected last. I used it to move equipment upstairs, but I prefer to use the stairs. I have someone coming out next week to inspect it."

When Knox didn't even pause at the second-floor landing, Salem wished she'd taken her heels off for the climb.

"The contractor just rewired the entire house. It was a complete mess for nearly a month, but they finished Monday and the cleaning crew came yesterday to put everything back in order. I just have to get all my equipment connected and running now." Knox's climbing speed and her ability to converse seemed to increase with her enthusiasm for her work.

Salem exercised often and was an avid biker, but she was struggling to keep up as Knox vaulted up the final flight of stairs. "Can you slow down? These heels aren't made for sprinting."

"Sorry." Knox slowed for the last two steps.

"It's okay. I think I picked up a few blisters stomping around the swamp."

The stairs ended at a landing with a single door.

"Open," Knox commanded, and Salem could hear a series of locks disengaging.

"Exactly what kind of business are we talking about?"

"I'm a software designer." Knox pointed to a keypad on the wall beside the door. "You can also get in by typing in the correct code, but the door locks every time it shuts and that gets a bit tedious for me. So I added voice recognition. My voice is the only one it recognizes, of course."

"Of course," Salem murmured, taking in the cavernous room. A thick canvas, painted the same medium-blue shade as the walls, floor, and ceiling, covered the dormer windows of the third floor. Several long tables were piled with computers and a tangle of Ethernet wires and electrical cords.

"I've converted this entire floor into a virtual-reality lab. Besides being expensive, my computers hold some classified government information, so the security system is separate from the house security. A central computer here in the house controls both systems."

"So, you're not just designing video games up here?"

"I still design a game every now and then, but only educational games to help kids learn. I've been involved in research and design of virtual-reality systems for the past six years."

"No blow-'em-up, shoot-'em-dead games?"

Knox stiffened and avoided Salem's gaze. She walked over to one of the tables and fingered a coil of wiring. "No. I don't like that kind of stuff." When she looked up, her eyes were shuttered and her earlier enthusiasm dimmed.

Salem instantly regretted her misstep and already missed the enthusiasm that lit up that beautiful face. "So, explain to me about virtual reality. Isn't that sort of like the hologram deck on those old *Star Trek* shows?"

"Yeah, sort of. In those old science-fiction movies, the simulator rooms were like futuristic video games. But in the real world, we're finding millions of ways to use virtual reality to help people."

"Like how? Are you going to feed people virtual food so that they don't actually eat calories and get fat?"

"I hadn't thought of that one."

Salem had meant it as a joke, but Knox seemed to be seriously considering the possibility. "You'd make a fortune and it could solve America's obesity problem."

"I'll put it on my list. Right now, I'm working on several medical programs."

"Can you tell me about them, or are they top secret?"

Knox smiled, the light returning to her eyes. "I'm developing a program that allows medical residents to operate on virtual patients. It would speed up their training by letting them practice a particular operation as often as they want, without the pressure of losing a real life if they make a mistake. The software also can deliberately trigger various complications so they can learn to troubleshoot during surgery."

"Wow."

"Yeah." Knox dug a pair of latex gloves out of a box and held them up so Salem could see the delicate mesh wiring embedded in the material. "See these wires? I can program them so a person wearing these gloves can actually feel the pressure of a virtual scalpel in her hands or the warmth and texture of a virtual human organ."

"You're kidding."

"No, really. The only thing I forgot was smell. The first students who tested the program said the thing that threw them off when they went into a real operating room was not being prepared for the smell."

"Can you do that?"

"I'm working on it, but there's a lot to consider. You've got disinfectant smells, intestinal smells, the scent of blood, body odor from the guy standing next to you who's been in surgery for twelve hours and hasn't showered. Lots of smells."

"I'm impressed."

Knox seemed to puff up at the compliment. "I also just signed a contract to develop a biomedical system that can scan a patient in a third-world country and relay information back to a doctor on the other side of the world for instant triage and diagnosis. But I doubt I can build a prototype up here. It might not fit in the elevator when I get it done. I'll probably convert the small barn into a mechanical lab."

"I thought you designed software. You build stuff, too? How many degrees do you have?"

"Oh, I don't have a degree in programming. I just picked it up. My degrees are physics, biomedical engineering, and a standard medical degree."

"A medical degree? As in, you're a doctor?"

"Yeah, I trained in surgery, but I'm better suited for the lab." Knox jammed her hands into her pockets and stared at the floor. "I don't like dealing with people all that much."

Salem marveled at the many changing faces of this intriguing woman. At first, she'd seemed aloof and reticent. But when she was in her element, like this lab, she was talkative and confident. Now she'd slipped into one of those moments when her sudden shyness made her seem very young and vulnerable. Salem wanted to hug her, but the one thing that remained constant was a huge personal space that hovered around Knox. She seemed to keep at least an arm's length of distance between them at all times. If Salem moved within touching distance, Knox would discreetly edge away.

"How old are you? I mean…I'll need to know your personal information for the paperwork."

"Twenty-eight."

"You must have been a regular Doogie Howser, huh?"

Knox shrugged. She pulled something from her pocket and held it out. "I put all the information you'll need, replacement costs, security specs, and stuff, on this thumb drive for you."

"Thanks. That'll make things a lot easier."

When she took the small memory stick from Knox's hand and her fingertips brushed against the soft skin of her palm, a strange tingling ran up her forearm. She looked up in surprise, and Knox averted her eyes and stuffed her hands into her jeans' pockets.

"Lots of static electricity with all these wires and equipment," she mumbled as she gestured toward the door. "We can take the elevator."

"What?"

"Your blisters. We can take the elevator back down. I need to show you the rest, but we'll drive my Jeep out to the barn."

"Right. The elevator sounds good."

The barn construction was actually within eyesight of the house, but Knox was acutely aware of Salem's effort not to limp from the elevator to the Jeep, and it felt imperative that she do everything possible to relieve her discomfort. The doctor part of her wanted to sit Salem in a chair and bathe those blisters in something numbing, then bandage her feet so the shoes wouldn't hurt any longer.

But her hand still tingled where Salem's fingertips had brushed her palm. More than that, she didn't even need to touch Salem to feel her sitting inches away in the Jeep. It was an unfamiliar but fascinating sensation. She gripped the steering wheel tighter to stop herself from leaning toward Salem.

"Um, my father bred Friesian horses years ago and I'm planning to rebuild the stable and his breeding program." Rather than walk through the barn, Knox drove slowly into the wide corridor of packed clay and stopped so Salem could see everything from her seat in the Jeep.

"The specs for the building are all on the flash drive. I'm rebuilding on the stone foundation of the original barn. All of the oak used for the frame and siding has been sealed with a special fire retardant, and a sprinkler system is being installed. Before we get any further with the construction, I wanted to know if insurers recommend any other fire-proofing steps."

"Wow. I can't say I've insured many barn structures, but it appears you have most everything covered. I can check, though, and get back with you tomorrow." Salem peered up at the open-beam construction. "No hayloft?"

"We'll store the hay in another building." Knox closed her eyes against the flashes of memory. Searing heat. Screaming horses. Flaming hay bales raining down from overhead.

"Knox, are you okay?"

She took a deep breath and opened her eyes. "Overhead lofts are a death trap if there's a fire," she said brusquely.

Knox abruptly threw the Jeep in gear and drove to a smaller barn a short distance away, then cut the engine and they sat in silence for a moment. Salem's energy had vibrated through her before, but now it washed over her in soothing waves. She could feel her question as loudly as if she'd spoken it.

"The first barn burned to the ground. We lost eight horses. I'm sure you saw that in my father's file. I was just a kid, but I'll never forget it."

Salem put her hand out as if to touch her, then stopped when Knox tucked her arm closer to her body. "I'm sorry. I haven't had time to review the file. This morning is the first time I've been in my father's office."

Knox frowned. "You should have told me. I could have waited a day. You haven't even had a chance to look in the desk drawers, and I've dragged you all the way out here."

Salem smiled. "Thanks to you, I've had an unforgettable adventure—"

"You called it an ordeal."

"An unforgettable adventure in which the tow-truck driver offered to service me as well as my car, and I toured an impressive virtual-reality lab and had a lovely drive around a historic estate. That's a hell of a lot better than sitting in the office, reviewing files my first day at work."

Knox was surprised to realize she, too, was enjoying their visit. She normally found it easier to be alone than around people because she didn't have to be careful. Salem did make her nervous, but comfortable at the same time. And she was enticingly attractive. Knox wanted to rub her cheek against that silky hair and brush her lips across the pulse that throbbed in Salem's neck. Heat scorched up her cheeks. Could she be more foolishly adolescent? She wasn't sure she should trust her tongue to speak, but Salem was looking at her for a response. "Uh, it was my pleasure."

Salem beamed at her and Knox was relieved that she must have said the right thing.

"My father built this smaller barn when the other one burned. This structure will become my biomedical shop after I move his horses into the new barn. I haven't researched the specs on that yet, so that information isn't on the flash drive. Right now, I just need to insure it as a stable."

"And you want to insure the horses? How many will you have?"

"Five. Dad's old gelding and two mares are here now, but I'll have my two mares shipped down here once the larger barn is finished. I only need to insure the mares. The gelding's only worth is sentimental."

"Don't you need a stallion to make babies? The place where I took riding lessons when I was a kid kept their two stallions in a barn separate from the mares. This small barn would be perfect for that."

Knox shrugged. "Stallions are too much trouble and the best Friesians are in Europe. It's easier to buy semen from overseas and have Doc Evan inseminate the mares. I just like raising the babies."

Salem jotted down a few more notes. "Any other structures?"

"Nothing worth insuring. The equipment barn is rented to several farmers who lease some of the estate's fields for growing corn and hay. But the building's old and they carry their own policies on the tractors and machinery they keep there. The hay barn's also too old to insure. It would be cheaper to just replace it."

Knox drove them back to the house and jogged inside to retrieve Salem's briefcase, but Salem followed and met her in the entryway.

"I guess I have what I need. If something's not on the flash drive, I'll call you. I'll check immediately and let you know if you need any further safety features for the barn. When I get the policies together, I'll give you a call to set up a time to sign them."

"Thanks." Knox handed over the briefcase, suddenly feeling anxious that Salem was leaving. She fidgeted, pushing her hands into her pockets and pulling them back out. She wanted, needed to say something, but what?

"Uh, maybe we could meet over lunch to sign the policies."

Yes! That's what she wanted to say. No! What if Salem thought she was asking for a date? What if the idea repulsed her? What if she made some lame excuse?

But Salem's eyes lit up. "That's a great idea."

"Yeah?"

"We're about the same age and both new in town. Well, you're not exactly new, but I am. Lunch would be lovely."

"Yeah. That's what I was thinking. Lovely."

"I'll see you soon then."

Knox didn't even see it coming. Suddenly, Salem's hand was on her bare forearm and every nerve in Knox's body focused on the fingers that gently squeezed her flesh and the energy that curled around hers.

Salem's eyes registered surprise just before she jumped at the popping sound overhead. Tiny bits of glass rained down on them from the chandelier, and Knox pulled Salem out of the way.

"Uh, must…must be a power surge or maybe a short in the new wiring," Knox said, nervously. "I'll get the contractor out right away to check his work again."

Salem eyed the light fixture. "Good idea."

Chapter Nine

Salem ignored the plaintive mewing outside the back door while she ground beans and spooned them into the coffeemaker. But when her two slices of bacon began to sizzle, the mewing grew loud and frantic, accompanied by the sound of tiny claws climbing the screen door.

She opened the door to find the kitten hanging eye-level, his eyes wide and his tail puffed out. Ignoring him and repeatedly returning him to the woods behind the house wasn't working. None of the neighbors claimed him and he was growing thinner every day.

She sighed. It looked like his persistence had earned him a home.

"Okay, you little bugger. I give up."

When she wrapped her hand around his tiny body to pry him from the screen, she could feel his ribs against her fingers.

"I don't have any cat food, but I can open some tuna for you. Do you like tuna?"

The kitten stared up at her and purred loudly.

"Okay. I'd say that's an affirmative."

As she retrieved a small can and dumped it onto a saucer, he climbed onto her shoulder and perched there like a bird, rubbing his cheek against hers.

"I guess if I'm going to keep you, I'll need to think of a name. Bugger. No, that reminds me of the British slang word for…um, never mind. You're too young to know what that means." She studied his gray tabby fur. "I refuse to name you something stupid like tiger or tabby." She mused further as he finished off the food and sat back to clean his face and paws. "Man, you really tucked into that food, didn't you little fellow? That's it. I'll call you Tuck."

He looked at her and let out a loud meow.

"You like that, huh? Tuck. I like it, too." She picked him up, filled a bowl with water, and set them both on the back step. "I guess now that I've fed you, I don't have to worry about you disappearing. I've got work today, so I'll meet you back here this evening with some proper kitty food."

That seemed agreeable with Tuck. He jumped up on a wooden bench at one end of the porch and sprawled in the sun to finish cleaning his paws.

Salem's first week in the office went quickly. Her father kept thorough records and, despite looking like she'd just stepped off the Grand Ole Opry stage, June was very efficient.

She had called Knox on Wednesday and advised her that the only precaution they hadn't discussed was the strength of her water source to the barn.

Knox promised to consult the local fire chief that same day and have a second well dug and a hydrant installed, if necessary to achieve the water pressure needed for fire hoses. Salem thought that was going a bit overboard for a barn, but she understood that her traumatic childhood experience was probably driving the extra measures.

She was still waiting to hear back on several inquiries she'd made for Knox's policies, but thoughts of her new client swirled in her head like the creamer she was stirring into her Monday morning coffee. Maybe she should give her a call, just to check in.

Knox answered on the second ring and Salem smiled at the familiar typing she could hear in the background. She pictured Knox hunched over her keyboard, pouring her genius into a virtual-reality program.

"I'm still working on finding the best policy for your computer lab," she said. "I'll probably have it ready for you to sign in a few days."

"That's fine. I'm sure I'm not your only client and you're probably busy settling in."

"It's no problem. How's the barn coming?"

"Nearly finished. They're starting on the stalls. I ordered them prefab, so they just have to fit them together and hang the doors. They might be done by the end of the week."

Salem suddenly realized she didn't want to hang up. She wanted to sit at her desk and listen to Knox's husky voice for just a few more minutes.

"I got a kitten," she said. She wondered if Knox planned to have cats in her barn to keep the mouse population down.

"Really? I've never had one. Where'd you get it?"

"Well, it kind of found me. It's a stray that's been hanging around the house. I finally fed it so now I guess I'm stuck with it."

"Good thing you didn't take it to the pound. They kill about eighty percent of the animals turned in there."

Salem shivered. "I could never do that."

"Good. That's good."

Salem felt inordinately pleased that Knox approved, but she'd run out of things to discuss and still needed to go to the grocery.

"Well, like I said, I'll call as soon as I get your policies ready. It shouldn't be more than a day or two. We can set up that lunch appointment."

"That would be great. I'll look forward to it."

Salem smiled. She was looking forward to seeing Knox again, too.

❖

The grocery was crowded with women replenishing their pantries and stocking up on gossip from the weekend. Salem was puzzling over the variety of cat food when the conversation of two women nearby caught her attention.

"I hear that she brought an electrician down here all the way from Washington, DC to rewire that old mansion, like people down here are too stupid to do it."

Were they talking about Knox? Salem picked up a bag of cat food and pretended to be reading the ingredients as she eavesdropped on the two women standing next to the dog-food displays.

"Didn't you hear? She's got some kind of top-secret government lab in her house. That's why her mama got kicked out and had to move to Florida. Those people who came down to work on the house were special secret agents," the woman with a beak-like nose said to her friend, who wore pink sweats. "Couldn't nobody local do it because they don't want us to know what's going on there."

"I thought she was a doctor."

"That's right! I remember now. Dr. Shepherd said she's some kind of genius and finished medical school when she was still a teenager. But I don't see her opening up an office here."

"Wouldn't nobody go if she did. Who knows what kind of experiments she might do on them." The pink woman narrowed her eyes. "You think you're getting a flu shot and, instead, you're getting some kind of experimental vaccine those government people sent down here."

"I'll bet she's doing some kind of experiments with killer germs and such."

Salem coughed to cover up the laugh she couldn't stop.

"Doc said she's rebuilding her daddy's barn that burned down years ago. I'll bet it ain't a barn at all. It's probably some type of hospital where she'll experiment on some poor animals."

A tow-headed boy ran up to the women, holding up two bags of cookies. "Mama, can I get these?"

"Choose one and put the other back," Beak-nose said. "And don't interrupt me when I'm talking." She turned back to Pink. "You could be right about that. There's already a barn where her daddy kept his horses. Why would she need another one?"

The boy interrupted again. "Ya'll talking about that Bolander woman? Granny says she's a witch. She was at the funeral and said that woman showed up and made the trees dance. I ain't never seen trees dance."

"You hush up. Granny's as crazy as a bedbug. Put those cookies in the cart and go get me a bag of potatoes."

The women glanced around uneasily, as if the boy had said something that would get them struck by lightning. They stared suspiciously at Salem, so she made her final selection and pushed her cart around the corner. She hurried down the next aisle to a spot where she could continue to eavesdrop and pretended to examine the feminine products in front of her. They didn't even bother to lower their voices, but took their own advice and moved on to the next piece of gossip.

"Did you hear who else just landed in town?"

"I have no idea."

"Franklin Lacey's girl."

"You don't say."

"Yep. June says he left his business to her and she's moved down here from Atlanta."

"So she's gonna run her daddy's business? I'll bet Lamar's not happy about that."

"Well, I don't know what's worse, having Lamar for an insurance agent or that girl."

"What'd you mean? What's wrong with her?"

"Don't you know why she never came down to visit her daddy?"

"Franklin never talked about it, but I heard it was a messy divorce. Maybe her mama wouldn't let her visit."

"That's not it at all. She's one of them," the woman lowered her voice to a stage whisper, "girls that play softball."

"No! And her daddy a pillar of the church."

"Well, she did grow up in sin city. Roy said that's why Franklin moved down here. He wanted to raise his daughter in a more wholesome environment, but his ex-wife refused and wouldn't let the girl come with him."

"Well, you can't really blame the child turning out like she did. She was just raised wrong. Maybe she'll get in a church down here and get straightened out."

"Maybe she came down here to start up a softball team in Oakboro."

"Lord, I hope not. This town is going to hell in a handbasket. Used to be you'd know every person you met on the street. Now, every time I turn around, some stranger's moving in—gays, people that might be witches—"

Salem had heard enough. She hurried through the checkout line and sat in her car fuming. After meeting Knox and seeing the account books of her father's business, she'd begun to consider staying in Oakboro. What the hell had she been thinking?

And what was that crap about trees dancing? Knox did have a sort of secretive air about her. But, really, a witch? Salem snorted. And, for their information, she'd never played softball in her life. Stupid hillbillies. No wonder Eve was messed up if the small town where she grew up was like this one.

❖

Knox waved good-bye to the fire chief and sprinted up the stairs to her computer.

A friendly fellow, he was younger than she expected, late thirties or early forties, and he came right out when she called. Maybe he was curious about what she was doing to the estate, or maybe being fire chief in a small town was boring and he was glad to have something to do.

At any rate, he'd been very helpful. He said another well was a gamble because, until you had sunk the pipe, you couldn't know how much water it would pump per minute.

He noticed the solar panels she was having installed on the roof of the barns and the house and suggested an equally "green" solution to her need for water. Dig the well, add a windmill to power it, and pump the water into an elevated retaining tank like farmers did in the old days before electric pumps, he said. The tank would hold more than enough water to fight a barn-sized fire, and its elevation would provide plenty of pressure for the fire hoses.

She spent the next hour researching windmills and retention tanks on the Internet, then placed her order with a company out of Tallahassee that promised to deliver and set it all up by the middle of next week.

She was delighted with the solution and couldn't wait to tell Salem about it.

Salem. Knox hadn't been able to stop thinking about her since she climbed into that muddy BMW and drove away the week before. Hearing her voice on the phone earlier that day had triggered a new round of fantasizing.

Her thoughts and energy were so out of control she had immediately unpacked the special anti-static mats she'd ordered for the lab and the wrist straps she wore to ground herself when she dismantled or built electronic equipment. The amount of static electricity her skin emitted depended on the level of energy that churned around her. It wouldn't do for her to blow a motherboard because of a random thought about soft skin and green eyes.

She hadn't needed to wear anti-static grounding straps for simple typing since puberty. Knox shuddered. That had been a horrible time.

Ryan had been the only other girl in the class. A year older than Knox, she was a mathematics genius. She also knew about Knox's unique ability and thought it was very cool.

Knox had hung on Ryan's every word and would do anything she asked. She got into trouble several times for using her gift to play Ryan's idea of a practical joke on the boys in the class. Their most frequent target was a boy named Jason, who was a couple of years older and liked to bully the younger kids.

The real problem began when Ryan lost interest in playing jokes on the boys and, instead, began to keep company with them rather than Knox.

Twelve-year-old Knox was jealous, and the hormones puberty was pumping into her system made her edgy. The maintenance crew was having a hard time keeping up with the exploding light bulbs every time her emotions blew a wave of energy through the room.

Then one day, Knox walked into the science lab and saw Ryan kissing a boy. Not just any boy. She was kissing Jason.

The Institute wouldn't soon forget the telekinetic tantrum that followed. Two days later, she woke up in a hospital room. Next to her bed sat an elderly Asian gentleman.

Master Kai was the first fellow telekinetic she'd met. Her energy was strong, but his was focused and gently held hers as he talked. He spoke to her about focus and control. And he quietly counseled her on the pitfalls of emotional relationships.

That day was the first of three years of training with Master Kai. Everyone has an aura of energy, he said, but most do not have the ability to control or project it. He taught her how to control her emotions and contain her energy.

She was closely observed for several years, but her watchers relaxed when they realized she had no sexual interest in boys.

She was so successful at Master Kai's lessons, she was able to convince the Institute instructors that puberty had stolen her gift like a child singer who loses the ability to sing high notes. Master Kai wasn't fooled, but it was her decision and he wouldn't expose her.

They both knew it was the only way she would be allowed to live her own life.

So she left the Institute when she was fifteen and, having already completed undergraduate work, she entered medical school. The women in those classes were at least six years older and rarely spoke to her. It didn't really matter. Mindful of Master Kai's warning about emotional relationships and fearful of losing control and exposing herself, she never socialized with the other students. She studied and tested out of courses before her classmates even got past the first chapters. She started her residency when they were just beginning their junior year.

By the time she finished, she was twenty-two years old, brilliant in the operating room and legendary in the biomedical engineering field. And she was totally ill-equipped and unprepared for casual social interaction.

So she retreated to a virtual operating room and worked.

She wasn't dead, of course. She watched television and movies, secretly mooning over certain actresses. She also had read several lesbian romances, and that's when her libido became intimately acquainted with her right hand. But those books kept her too stirred up, so she stopped reading and worked more.

Work had been enough. Until now. Until she rode her horse up to that dilapidated cottage and looked into those startling green eyes.

Thinking about Salem made Knox restless, so twitchy that she was in the barn and saddling one of her father's mares before she even realized why.

She guided her horse to a path that ran alongside the river and to the wooded property directly behind Salem's neighborhood. She hadn't meant to end up there, but the location of the house had been embedded in the back of her mind since she had hacked into Salem's GPS account to rescue her.

It was a fairly long ride and dusk began to settle around her, making her glad the broad path was even and the Friesian surefooted. She slowed the mare to a stop at the crest of a small hill. Although the woods were thin around her, the gathering darkness cloaked her sufficiently.

From her lookout, Knox realized Salem was sitting on her back porch, sipping from a glass of wine and petting a small kitten perched on her lap. Knox's urge to ride down there and join her was so strong, the mare shifted about in confusion. She took a deep breath to calm her energy and gentle the horse, because she didn't have the courage to act on her desire. She stared wistfully.

For the first time, Knox wished she had kissed a lot of girls. She wished she'd touched their bodies and learned how to bring them to ripping orgasms.

She desperately wished she wasn't twenty-eight years old and a never-been-kissed virgin.

Chapter Ten

Tuck was purring loudly and kneading Salem's lap with his little feet when he went suddenly still. Goose bumps ran down her arms as though something or someone had touched her. It reminded her of the static electricity in the air when lightning struck close by, but tonight's sky was cloudless.

Then she heard the hoofbeats, faint and rhythmic, and turned toward the shadowed woods. A thrill went through her as the dark figure of a horse and rider descended from the small knoll some distance from her house and disappeared among the trees. The high-stepping gait reminded her of Knox's horse and she wondered if it was her. Salem had found the dark-haired beauty with silver-gray eyes intruding on her thoughts a lot over the past few days.

Did Knox know what people in town said about her? Surely not. If she did, why would she have moved back here? She obviously had been living somewhere more progressive for a number of years. Had she forgotten about the cruelty of small-town prejudices and busybodies?

Salem's thoughts returned to the women at the grocery store. Bitches. Instead of leaving, she should have given them a piece of her mind. Her protective feelings toward her shy client surprised her.

Still, she should have said something. She shook her head in disgust. Right. Like that had really worked out well in Atlanta. Speaking up was exactly what landed her in this Georgia swamp her father had called home.

She was deep into her morose thoughts when the doorbell rang. Probably another nosy neighbor with a plate of brownies or an apple pie, stopping by to check out the prodigal daughter. Maybe she should buy a softball and glove to display in the living room. That'd give them something to gossip about.

She opened the door to a pleasant-looking woman holding a casserole dish wrapped in tinfoil.

"Hi."

"You must be Salem." The woman cocked her head and stared. "You have your father's eyes."

The appraisal made Salem a little uncomfortable. Or was it the comparison to her father? But the woman's tone held no accusation, so Salem pushed down her peeve with the grocery-store gossips. "Yes, I am. Would you like to come in?"

The woman stepped inside and handed the dish to her. "I'm Lucille. I didn't know how much you'd been able to settle in, so I brought you a chicken casserole. I won second place at the county fair with it last year."

"It smells wonderful and I haven't had dinner yet. Would you like to join me?"

"No, thank you, hon. It's nice of you to offer, but I've already eaten and I'm on my way to the ladies' Bible study at the church. I do have a few minutes to visit, though."

"Please sit down. I'll put this in the kitchen and be right back."

When she returned, the woman was perched nervously on the edge of the sofa. Salem sat in her father's recliner.

"Are you the same Lucille who baked those delicious cookies that made the house smell so wonderful when I arrived?"

Lucille smiled. "Guilty. Oh, I almost forgot." She fished around in her purse to extract a ring that held one key. "This is yours. I started to leave it on the table with the cookies, but I thought I'd better keep it until I knew for sure that you hadn't changed your mind about coming." She nervously glanced around the room. "I mean, June said you sounded a bit tentative about moving down here."

Salem took the house key and turned it over in her hands. "I'm not sure whether I'll stay or sell the business, but there's no rush to decide," she said absently. Why was she now uncertain about her earlier decision to sell, and why did this woman have a key to her father's house? Could she have been his housekeeper? Sleepover company? How could she ask without offending? "Are you a Realtor?"

Lucille lowered her eyes, her powdered cheeks flushed pink. "No. Your father and I kept company." She looked up, her gaze penetrating. "Not the kind of companion having a key to his house would imply. I had a key because sometimes he would get caught up at the office and I would come over and start dinner for the two of us."

"So you dated my father?"

"For eight years."

Salem was surprised. Who dated that long anymore without marrying or moving in together? Well, unless you were closeted gays. "Eight years? You're kidding."

"No, I'm not. I loved him. And he loved me as much as he could. We shared meals and chaste kisses, and we held hands. But your father was a man of faith and, despite the divorce, considered himself still married to your mother. We never slept together, and he never proposed."

"It's really none of my business. He was free to do what he wanted. I don't know you, Lucille, but it sounds like he used that as an excuse to string you along."

"I guess it may seem like that to some people, but it wasn't the case at all. He always made it clear his heart would only belong to her."

To her dismay, Salem's eyes began to fill with tears and she blinked them away.

Lucille patted her hand. "It's a shame you were estranged from him. He was a fine man and I wanted to tell you about our relationship before you heard the town gossips' version of what was between us."

Salem nodded, because she didn't trust her voice.

"Anyway, I didn't come by just to drop off a casserole and make you sad. I wanted to warn you about Lamar."

"Lamar? At the office?" She was relieved that Lucille had changed the subject.

"Yes." Lucille paused as if calculating what to say next. "Lamar is my son and I love him, but he's got a lot of his father in him. My Donnie was always trying to take shortcuts and coming up with schemes to make a lot of money. He was a truck driver and, in the end, skimping on tires and driving when he was tired cost his life."

"I'm sorry."

Lucille shrugged. "It was a long time ago. Lamar was only five years old, so he doesn't remember much about his daddy. Still, he's the same way. Always looking for a way to get rich quick. Franklin helped him pass the insurance exam and gave him a job, but he only tolerated Lamar for my sake. The boy comes and goes as he wants. Franklin should have fired him long ago."

"So you're here to tell me I should fire your son?" This was a little hard to believe.

"No. You should keep or fire him based on your best judgment of how he works for you. He knew Franklin wouldn't fire him because of me, and he took advantage of that fact. You don't have the same obligation, so I'm hoping he'll step up and do right for you."

"He hasn't been in the office much, and I've been busy working up a large commercial contract for a client."

"Well, I know June has an eye on him. But I need to tell you that Lamar had some crazy idea that the business would go to him after Franklin died. He's my boy, but I'm ashamed to say he hasn't proved himself trustworthy in the past. You should keep your eyes open where he's concerned."

"I appreciate it. It must be hard for you to tell me this." Salem gave Lucille's hand a quick squeeze. "And I promise to give Lamar a fair shake if he wants to shape up and do a good job."

Lucille's smile was sad. "I can see why your father was so proud of you. You've got a good head on your shoulders and a fair heart."

"My father didn't approve of me and thought I was headed straight to hell, Lucille. We haven't spoken in seventeen years. To tell the truth, I have no idea why he thought I'd move down here and take over his business."

"Yet here you are." Lucille patted her hand again. "Judge not lest ye be judged, young lady. Don't assume you know everything until you go through his things."

"Maybe *you* should do that. I'm sure his belongings mean something to you. My father was just another stranger to me," she said.

"Oh, honey. I think you'll find he isn't the stranger you think." Lucille rose from her seat. "May I show you something before I leave?"

Frowning, Salem stood, too. "You know, I'm really tired and you're going to be late for your meeting."

"Please. It'll only take a minute."

Salem relented and stepped back to let Lucille lead the way into her father's study. Lucille pulled a shoebox from the top shelf of the closet and handed it to her.

"This box is full of letters written to you by your father. I'm sure you know about the ones that he mailed because you returned them unopened. After the fifth or sixth returned letter, he would write one and then take it to the post office where I work and ask me to postmark it without mailing it. He wanted a time stamp that showed when he wrote it." Lucille's eyes filled with tears. "We knew his surgery was risky. He had suffered a massive heart attack and there was a lot of damage. Before they took him into the operating room, he made me promise to be sure you found these. What you do with them is up to you."

Salem stared at the box in her hands. Likely more sermons about homosexuality.

"Don't cheat yourself by refusing to read them," Lucille warned her, apparently reading Salem's expression. She turned to go.

"Lucille, wait." Salem hesitated, suddenly unsure of what she had wanted to say. "Uh, thanks for the chicken casserole and the cookies. I'll return your dish later if you'll write down your address."

Lucille smiled warmly. "You can drop the dish by the post office. Or just come by to chat. Read those letters, hon."

❖

The casserole was so good, Salem ate two helpings. Then she poured herself another glass of wine and considered what to do next. The cable television wouldn't be hooked up until tomorrow. She had three or four unread books on her e-reader but was too restless to read.

Instead, she wandered into her father's room. What was she going to do with all his stuff?

She opened the closet and ran her hand down the sleeve of a dark-blue suit. Was that a hint of…she lifted the cloth to her nose. The faint scent of her father's cologne was just as she remembered it. As a little girl, she'd loved to sit in his lap while he read to her from whatever murder mystery he was enjoying. It didn't matter that the content wasn't on her age level. She would close her eyes and lay her head against his strong chest. His spicy scent and deep voice vibrating against her cheek made her feel safe and loved.

Loved. He hadn't loved her. He had loved the daughter he wanted her to be.

She closed the closet. She'd throw all his clothes into some trash bags and donate them to charity. She didn't have any use for them.

The oak four-poster bed and dresser were beautiful antiques. Maybe she'd keep those.

She wasn't surprised that some shelves built into one wall were cluttered with books. Her father was an avid reader. She was shocked, however, to find a handful on homosexuality. She touched the spines, tracing her fingers over the titles. She didn't recognize any of them, but she wasn't into nonfiction. And she didn't need a book to understand what felt as natural to her as breathing.

One title read *Help, My Kid is Gay*! Another read *Choice or Genetics*?

She snorted. Probably got them at a Baptist bookstore to try to figure out how to "cure" her. He probably kept them in his bedroom, rather than on the bookshelf in the living room, so nobody would know he had a gay daughter. The thought left a sour taste in her mouth.

If he didn't want people to know about her, why leave his business to her? Was he clinging to the ridiculous idea that a change of residence could alter her sexual orientation?

She moved to the dresser and touched the framed photograph of her and her mother. Did he pray for their souls every day? It pissed her off to think he might have.

Taking a big swallow of her wine she walked down the hallway to her father's home office. The walls were covered with photographs of her and her mother. Some were duplicates of pictures her mother had in her house: Salem holding up a volleyball trophy, Salem grinning next to her insurance-broker certification, Salem celebrating her twenty-first birthday. Had her mother sent copies to him?

But she also discovered pictures she'd never seen before, photographs of her high-school and college graduations. Her mother was in some of the pictures with her, so she couldn't have taken them. Had he been there? Why did he bother going to her graduations if he was too ashamed of her to make his presence known?

Her eyes burned and her throat tightened. She had always been Daddy's girl while she was growing up. He had filled her life with love when she was small. Now every thought of him was laced with anger and resentment. She hated her father. Didn't she?

She brushed away her tears as if she could clear away her confused feelings. What the hell was she still doing in this tiny, probably ninety-percent evangelical backwater town? She kept asking herself that question and still didn't have a good answer.

She went to the kitchen to refill her wine glass and slip out into the tepid night. When her eyes adjusted to the twilight, she scanned the knoll for the horse and rider. She smiled despite her foul mood, thinking of Knox astride her dark horse as it high-stepped across the clearing toward her.

There was her answer.

Chapter Eleven

Salem hit the Print key one more time and began to gather the papers and tuck them into her briefcase. She had received the last quote updated with the information about the windmill and water tower. She tapped the screen on her phone, not stopping to think why Knox was her number-one speed dial.

"Hello?"

"Hey, it's Salem. I've got the last of your quotes together. If you're not busy, I'll drive out and go over them with you."

"You don't have to do that. I can come into town. Did you change your mind about meeting for lunch?" Knox sounded disappointed.

"Actually, the weather's so nice, I thought I could pick up some fried chicken from the diner and maybe we can lunch on your terrace."

"Yeah, that's a great idea. If you aren't busy, we could go riding after I sign the contracts. Uh, that is if you'd like to."

Salem smiled at the hesitation in Knox's voice. For a woman so beautiful and intelligent, she seemed adorably unassuming. "That would be wonderful."

"Excellent. Okay, then. I'll see you in a few minutes?"

"I'm going to swing by the house to change into jeans, then I'll pick up the chicken and be right out."

"Okay. Um, I found a recipe for lemonade and made some. It tastes a lot better than my first attempt."

"That's so sweet. See you soon."

Salem ended the call and pumped her fist in the air. "Yes." What was the use of owning your own business if you couldn't take off work when you wanted? An afternoon of riding sounded really good. Spending that time with Knox? Even better.

❖

Salem hummed as she drove down the two-lane blacktop leading out of town. Lamar was still a no-show at the office, but June had assured her she'd be happy to handle any pressing calls that afternoon.

She was reconsidering her initial assessment of June, who was a very capable office manager and really sweet. The secretary she'd had in Atlanta would have been on her way to the boss's office right now, anxious to tell him that Salem was taking an unscheduled afternoon off. June just shooed her out the door and ordered her to forget work for the rest of the day.

She was filled with anticipation but told herself she was looking forward to riding those beautiful horses.

No matter. It wasn't like she was packing a U-Haul and going after Knox. She just needed a friend and, apparently, Knox felt the same way. Nothing wrong with having friends. Right?

Hell, she didn't even know if Knox was gay. But her gut told her she was. And if she was wrong, it'd be a damn shame. She recalled those arresting eyes, and heat rose up her neck at the thought of kissing those full lips.

Stop. Knox was a client. And Salem was pretty sure she wouldn't settle in Oakboro. So she had to stop thinking of Knox as anything other than a potential friend. She had to stop—

"Shit!"

Salem slammed on brakes, thanking the gods that the BMW's tires gripped the blacktop as she jerked the steering wheel to whip around a large dog standing in the middle of the roadway, sniffing something dead. The dog didn't appear to hear her and, although her car skidded to a near stop, the front fender still caught him on the back leg and tossed him to the pavement.

She jumped out, but the German shepherd scrambled up and limped into the woods on three legs.

"Wait! Here, doggy." She hesitated at the edge of the woods, afraid she'd get lost again. "Shit!" She needed help.

❖

Taking the steps two at a time wasn't fast enough, so Knox slid down the banister of the staircase like she had when she was a child. Tires screeching in the circular drive and then frantic pounding at the front door were a sure sign of something wrong.

She yanked the door open and found Salem, pale and shaking.

"I need help. You're a doctor, right? A real doctor?"

"Yeah. A real doctor." Knox led her to a chair in the foyer and grabbed Salem's wrist. Her pulse was racing, and Knox had to consciously stop her heart from matching the pace. "Sit down and take a few deep breaths. Are you hurt anywhere?"

Salem shook her head. "No, not me. I hit a dog. With my car. I'm sure he's injured, but he went into the woods. I need to find him."

"A dog?"

"On the road, about a mile back." Salem clutched Knox's shoulders. "You've got to help me find him."

"Let me get a first-aid kit."

"Don't you have a black doctor's bag?" Salem frowned. "I thought every doctor had a black bag full of medical stuff."

Knox would have laughed if they hadn't been in emergency mode. "Come on. I'll call Doc Evan while you drive." She grabbed a backpack filled with medical supplies from the coat closet. "How big was the dog?"

"I think it was a German shepherd. I saw blood on the road, and when he ran off, he was holding up one of his hind legs like he couldn't put weight on it."

They jumped into the car and Knox tapped a number on her phone. She put it on speaker so Salem could hear.

"Oakboro Veterinary Clinic."

"This is Knox Bolander. I've got an emergency, a dog hit by a car. Is Doc Evan in the office?"

"He's handling large-animal calls this afternoon, so he just left. Can't be more than two blocks away. Hold on, I can get him on the other line."

Salem pulled over just as Doc's assistant, Tony, came back on.

"Doc says to hang up. He's got your cell number and is going to call you."

"Okay, thanks." Knox pointed to spots of still-bright blood. The phone rang just as they hopped across the ditch and headed into the woods.

"Where are you?" Doc said.

"On highway 97 going out of town, about a mile before you get to my place," Knox answered. "Look for a BMW parked on the shoulder. We're headed into the woods now. Looks like the dog's bleeding, so I'm hoping it didn't go far."

"Call me if you find it before I find you."

"Will do." Knox ended the call and picked up the backpack. Without thinking, she took Salem's hand and squeezed it. "Don't worry. Do you want to wait here?"

Salem, her color returning, shook her head vigorously. "No. I'm coming with you."

They followed the spots of blood for only a short distance before they found him. The beautiful black-and-tan shepherd lay panting, his long pale tongue lolling against large white teeth. Knox approached cautiously.

"Hey, boy. Looks like you've run into a little trouble," she crooned to him. "How about letting us have a look."

The dog whined and watched Knox as she knelt close behind him.

"Be careful," Salem said. "He might bite you."

Knox carefully laid her hand on his back along his spine and the dog seemed to relax, dropping his head to the ground. "Punch the two on my phone to call the doc."

Salem put it on speaker and Doc picked up on the first ring.

"Hey, Doc. We found him. It's a German shepherd, probably about eighty pounds. He's a little shocky. I've got some stuff with me, saline and Banamine. He's got a cut on his right hind, and it definitely looks broken just below the knee."

"Hold off. I'm pulling up now."

Salem turned toward the road. "Over here," she shouted when she saw him climb out of his truck.

Doc waved, then trotted toward them with a medical bag and a lightweight stretcher of molded plastic under his arm. He groaned when he reached them. "God damn it. I've told that idiot Barnes not to let this dog run free." He knelt and began pulling things from his bag.

"You recognize him?" Salem asked.

"This is Guardian. He's got great bloodlines, but his owner unfortunately doesn't. He's about the stupidest man in the world." He edged toward the dog and reached out cautiously. "Hey, old buddy. Got yourself in a mess here, didn't you?"

"He was just standing there in the road sniffing at something when I came around the curve," Salem said, wringing her hands nervously. "I hit the brakes so hard the tires were squealing, but he didn't even notice or try to get out of the way."

"He's deaf."

"Deaf?" Knox was surprised. Shepherds weren't one of the breeds prone to deafness.

"Yeah. His sorry owner let him get such a bad infection in both ears, he lost his hearing. That's one reason I've warned him about letting him run free."

Guardian whined and licked at Doc's hand as he checked his gums.

"He doesn't look that shocky."

"He's better than he was when we found him."

Doc's gaze traveled to the hand Knox still held against Guardian's spine. "Pressure point?"

"Something like that," Knox muttered, casting a glance at Salem.

He nodded and prepared a syringe. "I'm going to sedate him a little, so you can let go and help me get him on the stretcher."

He administered the drug and carefully recapped and stowed the syringe in his bag before holding it out to Salem. "Could you carry this for me while Knox and I load him up in the truck, Miss—"

"Salem Lacey. Will he be okay?" she asked anxiously, taking his bag and shouldering Knox's pack, too.

Doc studied her face. "So you're Franklin's girl."

"Yes, Franklin Lacey was my father," she said.

Knox looked up, surprised at Salem's stiff answer.

But Doc just nodded. "I think old Guard will be fine, Ms. Lacey, but we need to get some X-rays before I can say for sure."

He and Knox carefully lifted Guardian onto the stretcher and carried him to the veterinary truck, where they slid the stretcher onto the backseat of the crew cab.

"Knox, you need to ride beside him to make sure he doesn't roll off onto the floor," Doc said.

Knox turned to Salem. "Do you want to follow us?"

"I'll be right behind you."

When they arrived at the clinic, a slender, handsome blond held the door open as they carried Guardian into the clinic.

"Aw, man. Not Guard."

"We need to set up the surgery room, Tony," Doc said.

"I figured that much from the call earlier. It's ready and I rescheduled your two afternoon appointments." He sighed. "And I called Jeff to let him know I'll be late."

"You don't have to stay."

"Are you sure? I mean, you know I'll stay, but we've got reservations in Tallahassee for dinner."

"It's your fifth anniversary. Bad luck to miss that one. Trust me. I missed a lot of birthday and anniversary dinners with my wife that I wish I could get back now that she's gone," Doc said. "Knox will give me a hand. It'll do her good to use that medical degree for something other than pecking away on those computers. You boys go have a good time."

"Thanks, Doc. You're the best. What can I do for you before I head out?"

"You can show Ms. Lacey—"

"Salem. Please, just call me Salem."

"You can show Salem here to my office, where she can be comfortable while Knox and I fix up Guard. Get her some crackers and a soda, too. She looks a little pale."

"Oh, our lunch is in the car. I guess I should bring it inside so it doesn't spoil."

After they watched Doc and Knox disappear down the hallway with Guardian, Salem retrieved their lunch basket from the car and Tony showed her to a large comfortable office that, in addition to the scuffed oak desk, had a full-sized refrigerator and sitting area with a long leather sofa, a recliner, and a television.

"Wow. You could live in this office."

"He practically does live here since his wife died. There's a bathroom and shower through that door over there. I can't tell you how many mornings I've come in here early and found him snoring in that recliner with the television still on. He needs to meet somebody, but he's such an old grump I don't know who'd have him."

"Well, I don't want to keep you."

"I've got a little time. Jeff isn't expecting me for another hour."

"How long do you think they'll be in there?"

"It all depends on how much damage they have to repair." He looked at her sympathetically. "Maybe a couple of hours. I'm sure Doc would give Knox a ride home if you don't want to wait that long."

Salem ran a shaky hand over her face. "No. I want to stay. I'll just put this lunch basket in the fridge and thumb through a few of these *National Geographic*s." She'd noticed a tall pile of them next to the recliner. "I've got enough in that picnic basket for three, and they'll probably be hungry when they're done."

Tony pointed to the sofa. "You sit," he said sternly. "Doc's right. You look a little pale." He rummaged in the refrigerator and held up a can of soda. "I've got you pegged for a Diet Coke kind of girl."

Salem nodded as he handed over the cold can and a package of cheese crackers and parked his butt on the desk. It was obvious he wouldn't leave until he made sure she ate something.

"So, it's your anniversary, huh? You guys have been together five years?"

Tony smiled. "Actually, we've been together going on eight years. But five years ago, we flew to Canada and got married. Jeff was born there and has dual citizenship."

"Really? How'd he end up in Oakboro?"

"He's a writer. He came down here to visit a friend in Panama City and fell in love with the South. He says there're a million stories here. We met in Tallahassee and fell in love, so he never went back to Canada."

"Is he famous? Would I recognize his name?"

"Probably not. He's not *New York Times* best-seller famous, but he makes a good living writing stories about a kick-ass woman detective under a female nom de plume for a mainstream publisher. He also writes gay romances for a LGBT publisher, just for his own pleasure."

"I'd love to meet him."

"He's a real romantic, and incredibly handsome." He placed his hand over his heart and pretended to swoon.

Salem laughed. The food and the relaxing conversation were, indeed, helping her feel better. "You wouldn't be a little biased, would you?"

He grinned. "What about you? This little accident seems to have interrupted your lunch date with Miss Hottie Bolander in there."

Salem nearly choked on the soda she was swallowing. After a few coughs and several pats on her back from Tony, she shook her head. "I was going out to the Bolander place because I have some insurance contracts that need her signature."

"Yeah, my insurance agent always brings over a picnic basket full of fried chicken, too, when he needs me to sign something."

Busted. Salem's cheeks heated and Tony laughed. She narrowed her eyes. "What makes you think I'm gay?"

"Girl, you're all your daddy ever talked about."

"Yeah, I'll just bet he did."

Tony looked surprised at her reaction. "Really. He and Doc were fishing buddies, and Jeff went with them sometimes. He likes to fish, too. I went once but was bored to tears. Your daddy knew about Jeff and me and that Doc has no problem with us. So I guess he felt comfortable enough to talk about you around us. He loved Jeff's mysteries. He bought every one of them."

This didn't make sense. It didn't sound like the father who deserted her. She was turning this new information over in her head when Tony jumped up from his seat.

"Oh my God, I completely lost track of time. I've still got to shower and get dressed for my big night." He squeezed her shoulder. "I can't wait to tell Jeff I met you. We definitely must have you and Miss Hottie over for dinner."

He started to leave, but turned back for one last word. "Your daddy didn't like that politician woman you were seeing. He didn't believe you could trust someone who couldn't be honest about herself."

Chapter Twelve

Knox tied off the last stitch and Doc turned off the anesthesia. They had set the dog's lower hind leg and cast it before sewing up the cut on Guardian's hip. The fine bones of his lower leg had been splintered, but Knox deftly pinned the pieces together with tiny metal screws.

"Appreciate your help," Doc said. "I'm getting arthritis in my hands and handling those little bitty screws is just too hard these days. I probably would have driven him to a surgery center in Tallahassee."

Knox smiled. "Anytime. Although I'm pretty sure my malpractice insurance wouldn't cover working on dogs."

"You want to explain to me what you were doing when I got to y'all out there in the woods?"

Knox shrugged and pretended to be checking Guardian's cast. "Not sure what you're talking about."

"You don't have to hide it from me, honey. I'm saying that dog didn't look like he was in pain at all."

"It's hard to explain how I do it, but it has the effect of a spinal block…sort of interrupts the electrical impulses that travel along the spine."

Doc nodded. "You could do a lot of good things with that gift, kiddo."

Knox crossed her arms over her chest and scowled. She didn't want to be different. She wanted to be like everybody else. She wanted to have friends and, since she'd met Salem, she'd been wondering what it would be like to have someone to share her life. "If the Institute knew I could still do that stuff, I probably wouldn't be standing here right now. My life wouldn't be my own. You can't tell anyone, Doc Evan. Not a single soul."

"Calm down, girl. Your secret's safe with me." He gathered Guard gently in his arms. "I'm going to put him to bed in the back so he can sleep off the anesthesia. You should go check on your pretty friend."

❖

Knox stood in the doorway of the office and took a moment to gaze at the angel who had fallen asleep on Doc's couch. Salem was open and outgoing. Not like her. But seeing her face relaxed in slumber, she realized that Salem, too, held back a part of herself when she was with people. What could have caused that wariness in this gorgeous woman? Was she as lonely as Knox felt?

During their earlier crisis, she had held Salem's hand without thinking. She closed her eyes and tried to recall how those slender fingers felt curled around hers. She wished she'd taken time to implant in her memory the sensation of Salem's warm skin. But she didn't dare touch her now that she had time to think about it. She knelt next to the couch.

"Salem," she said softly.

The thick lashes fluttered and opened to reveal hazy green eyes. Knox leaned closer.

"We're all done. He's going to be fine."

Salem sat up and rubbed her face. "God, I didn't mean to fall asleep. What time is it?"

"About two thirty. I don't know about you, but I'm starving."

"I've got our lunch in the fridge. There's more than enough for Doc Evan, too."

"Somebody say something about food?" Doc appeared in the doorway and Knox stood quickly.

"Cold fried chicken, potato salad, and pecan pie," Salem said. She smiled sheepishly at Knox. "The waitress at the diner said you liked pecan and she threw it in for free. She said it was a thank-you for remembering Max when you needed a tow truck. I don't think she realized it was my car that Max had to pull out of the mud."

"Well, I wouldn't have called her if I'd known Max would offer extra services," Knox muttered.

Salem grinned. "It was easy enough to turn down and didn't offend me, so don't hold that against her."

"Y'all can talk all day if you want, but I'm digging into this chicken." Doc swept aside the papers on his desk and unfolded a red-and-white-checkered tablecloth to cover it. "Lunch is served."

They spread the food out on the desk and filled their paper plates, then Doc settled in his recliner and she and Salem sat next to each other, but not too close, on the couch.

"Are you going to call Guard's owner?" Knox asked. The man didn't sound like he deserved to own such a fine dog.

"Can he be charged with animal cruelty or something for letting a deaf dog run loose?" Salem asked.

"It's not against the law to let dogs run loose in the country, deaf or not. And there's no law that keeps idiots and mean people from owning animals. It's a shame, but that's the way it is," Doc said. "I believe, however, I can do something about Guard. But first, I've got to know something. Either one of you want a really nice German shepherd?"

Knox looked up from her chicken. "You serious?"

"I believe I can talk Barnes into givin' him up, but I need to know he'll have a home if I do."

Salem frowned. "I've never had a dog and I just adopted a stray kitten. In fact, I need to bring him in for whatever vaccinations you give cats."

"I'll take him," Knox said quickly. "I've always wanted a dog like him. I'll pay any price he wants if he'll sell him."

"Don't think you'll have to pay a penny. Just let me make a call." He dug the phone out from under the tablecloth and consulted a file before punching in the number. Holding his finger to his lips for them to be silent, he put the phone on speaker.

"Barnes. It's Dr. Evan Shepherd over at the veterinary clinic."

"Hey, Doc. I heard you and Turner went deep-sea fishing out of Panama City and didn't catch a thing. Turner's still talking about how much money it cost him just to float out there all day. Says he could have stayed home if all he was going to do was drink beer."

"I wish he'd stayed home, too. He ran his mouth the entire time. That's probably what scared the fish off."

A loud guffaw sounded through the speaker. "How you doing these days?"

"I'm good, but you're not going to be when I tell you what I'm calling about. You know that big shepherd you've got? Well, he was running loose again and got hit on the highway."

"Damn. I reckon he's dead then. My daddy always said any dog stupid enough to stand in the road didn't deserve to live. I'll sure miss the stud fees I got from him. Shoulda kept a puppy from the last litter."

"Thing is, he ain't dead. But his leg was tore up pretty bad so I had to get some help from a specialist. It's gonna cost ya."

"Cost me? How much? I just spent a bundle on a red convertible for my wife. Heh. The 'thank you' I get every time she drives it is worth every penny."

Knox could almost hear the man's leer.

"You should have called me before you did all that. I'd have told you to just put him down."

"Yeah, I probably should have called first but knew what you'd say, and I wasn't going to put down a good dog."

"How much money we talking about?"

"Don't know yet. I'll have to tally it up. A couple thousand for sure."

"Well then, looks like you've got yourself a dog, Doc. Ain't no way I'm going to pay that…unless…how about I just let you have his stud fees until the bill's paid up?"

Doc winked at them. "I could take his stud fees as payment, but here's the problem. The car that hit him busted his nuts. You won't be getting any more puppies out of him."

"Damn. Then I don't care what you do with him. Keep him or kill him. He's your dog now."

"If that's what you want. I can probably find him a home."

"You do that."

"Even though he won't be good for breeding, I still need his papers to transfer ownership."

"Drop by the office and ask my secretary to dig them out for you. And, Doc, call me next time you go deep-sea fishing."

"I'll do that." Doc punched a button to end the call and grimaced at the phone. "When hell freezes over." He smiled. "Looks like you've got yourself a dog. I better keep him here a day or two until he's getting around on three legs okay. I'll let you know when you can pick him up."

They finished their meal while Doc regaled them with funny stories about his clients and their pets. Then Salem and Doc began to put the food away, and Knox slipped down the hallway to the kennel room where Guard lay awake on a thick foam pad. He rose up on his chest and thumped his tail when she approached.

She held out her hand for him to sniff. "Hey, boy. Guess what? When you get better, you're coming home with me. I have lots of fields to run in that aren't near the road, and I have horses and a big house. Guardian studied her face as she spoke. "Oh, I forgot you can't hear. Maybe you read lips, huh? How's that leg feel?" He whined and licked her hand. "Hurts, I guess. I might be able help you with that."

Knox rubbed her hands together, then laid one on his hip and the other on his cast. She closed her eyes and concentrated on the warm energy radiating through her hands. When she opened her eyes a few minutes later, Guardian was sleeping again. She ran her hands through his soft fur. Unlike some shepherds that were mostly tan, Guard's saddle of black dominated his coat, running from head to tail. He was very handsome.

"So, that Karate Kid stuff really works?"

Knox was startled by the soft voice behind her. How long had Salem been standing there?

"What?"

"What you did with your hands. It was like *The Karate Kid* movie where the old man rubbed his hands together and laid them on the boy's knee to make it better so he could finish the tournament."

"Oh, yeah. I learned it from Master Kai. He taught mathematics and other stuff at the Institute, where I went to school." Knox stood. "I didn't realize you were watching. I feel a little silly."

"It's not silly if it helps. You'll have to explain how it works sometime."

She searched Salem's face for any sign of the uneasiness she usually encountered when people began to suspect she was different, but saw nothing but curiosity and sincere interest. "Uh, okay. I'll try."

"Are you ready to go? I probably should check back in with the office after we go over your paperwork."

"Sure." She squatted next to Guardian one more time, but refrained from touching him again so he wouldn't wake. "I'll come back for you, boy. Doc Evan will take care of you until I do."

❖

Salem drove Knox home and they spread the insurance paperwork out on her dining-room table to review. The contracts totaled up to a tidy sum, so she suggested that Knox consult with another broker for comparison. But Knox firmly declined, signed on every line Salem pointed out, and wrote a check to cover the rest of the year and another full year.

She paused at the front door as Knox walked her out. They had decided against a horseback ride after all the excitement, but Salem was reluctant to leave. "Thanks for being so great and coming to my rescue again."

Christ, Knox was stunning when she smiled.

"It's not a problem. I know it was upsetting for you, but I'm getting a great dog out of the deal and lunch was still fun."

"Why do you call him Doc Evan instead of Dr. Shepherd?"

"He and my father were friends from the time I was a kid. He's just always been Doc Evan to me. Tony and a lot of people just call him Doc."

"I've got an appointment with him in the morning to get my kitten vaccinated."

"What kind is he?"

"I'm sorry?"

"The kitten. What breed?"

Salem chuckled. "I thought at first he was just an ordinary gray tabby, but now I think he's part parrot. He likes to climb up and perch on my shoulder when I'm washing dishes or reading."

"Sounds cute."

"You should come by the house some evening and meet him. We could throw some steaks on the grill or something."

"That would be nice," Knox said softly.

They held each other's gaze for a long moment before Knox looked away, her cheeks coloring. Whatever was happening between them, something told Salem not to push.

She held up her briefcase. "I'll get these activated first thing tomorrow."

"Thanks. I appreciate all your work on them."

"Don't worry. I'm collecting a big fat fee on these babies."

"You earned it." One corner of Knox's full lips turned up in a half smile, and Salem had to force herself to resist kissing her.

"Well, I better go. Maybe we can go riding another time?"

"How about Saturday morning, before it gets too hot?"

"That would be wonderful. What time?"

"Around nine?"

Salem ran her eyes over Knox's long frame. Again, she had to hold herself back from wrapping her arms around that lean body. But, while Knox had touched her freely several times earlier that day, she now stood two steps away with her arms clasped across her rib cage, her do-not-enter-personal-space signals firmly in place.

Salem smiled warmly. "Nine is perfect."

Chapter Thirteen

Salem was still humming happily when she strolled into the office.

June looked up and smiled. "Well, things must have gone well out at the Bolander place. Did you girls have a good ride?"

Salem waved as she headed down the hallway to her office. "Oh, we didn't get to go riding. I had a terrible accident on the way there," she said over her shoulder.

June jumped up from her desk and followed hot on Salem's heels. "Are you okay, honey? You're not hurt, are you?"

"I hit a dog. It was awful." Salem's smile dimmed for a moment, then returned after she described what happened to the dog. "His leg is broken, but Knox fixed it right up. She's a trained surgeon, you know."

June cocked her head, seeming amused. "Robert mentioned it a few hundred times when he came by to collect your father for their Wednesday golf game. He was very proud of her."

"Our fathers were friends?"

"Very good friends. They would be pleased that you two girls are getting to know each other."

Salem pulled the signed contracts from her briefcase. "We have a date to go riding Saturday morning."

The minute the words were out of her mouth, she froze inside. Had her father also told June she was gay? Was she revealing something about Knox that she shouldn't? Heck, she'd just assumed

Knox was gay. Maybe June would just think she meant "date" as in "appointment."

But June smiled broadly and patted her on the arm. "That's wonderful, honey. Max says she's very attractive."

Salem hesitated, taking in June's flowered dress and heavily sprayed hairdo. Surely she didn't mean that the way Salem heard it. But before she could decide how to respond, the phone rang and June answered it at Salem's desk.

"Good afternoon, Lacey Insurance. How can I help you? Lamar said he wouldn't be back in the office today, but let me put Ms. Lacey on the phone. Hold on, please."

June put the caller on hold and reached for the contracts Salem held in her hand. "It's Raeford Price. I'll bring his file right back and fax those contracts off for you while you see what he wants."

Salem nodded and settled into her chair to take the call.

"Mr. Price. This is Salem Lacey. What can I do for you today?"

"I sure was sorry about your daddy," Raeford said. "My family's done business with his office ever since he opened it, and we were ushers at church together. He was a good man."

"Thank you. I appreciate that. I hope you'll continue to do business with us."

"That's what I'm calling about. I own a construction business and my son started his own flooring business as a spin-off. That boy, Lamar, wrote up a policy for Junior a couple of years back. He hasn't had a claim against it yet, but somebody got hurt on the job yesterday, and I told him I'd call it in for him because he has to fill in at the work site until his man can come back to work."

"What type of accident are we talking about?"

"Durned nail gun misfired and put a nail right though the boy's hand. He'll be okay, but there's medical bills to pay and short-term disability. Doctor says it'll be a few months before he can lay floors again."

June reappeared and laid a thin file on Salem's desk marked Price Flooring. Salem quickly paged through it and frowned. She didn't see much in the folder, just a policy on the contents of the business's office and equipment. No medical or workman's comp policy. Who would run a business without those policies?

"Some things seem to be missing from the file in the office, Mr. Price. Perhaps Lamar has another folder somewhere."

"Junior's got copies if that dummy's lost his. I swear I don't know why Franklin put up with him."

"I'm sure we'll find our copies. But tell your son to relax. If you can fax over the medical bills, I'll personally take care of this for him."

"I appreciate that. You're a chip off the old block."

Salem hung up the phone and paged through the file again. Who would write such an incomplete policy? Something wasn't right here and she had a bad feeling about it.

The door to Lamar's office was closed and, even though June had said he wasn't in, she knocked sharply. When she didn't get an answer she tried the door, but it was locked. She banged on the door in frustration. "Damn it. Sorry little bastard." The incomplete folder irritated her because she couldn't tolerate sloppy bookkeeping. But the locked door did more than irritate her. It royally pissed her off.

She went back to her desk and looked up the cell number for Lamar. It went right to voice mail.

"Lamar, this is Salem Lacey. I need to see you in this office at nine sharp tomorrow morning. If you have another appointment, postpone it. This is important." She slammed the receiver back into its cradle. It was time for a sit-down with this guy. She picked the phone up again and buzzed June's desk.

"I just called a locksmith to get that door open for you," June answered before Salem could say a word.

"Thank you. You read my mind."

June chuckled. "Not exactly. I could hear you cursing all the way out here."

❖

Salem wanted to rub her tired eyes, but opted for a few drops of eye lubricant so she wouldn't smear her mascara and eyeliner. She'd had little more than four hours of sleep after working until two in the morning to dig through the mess that Lamar called an office. Many of the policies he had written were missing coverage that should be standard. Even more alarming, those policies were always paid in cash. That was unusual in the insurance business and surely should have raised an auditor's eyebrows.

She was standing in the office's small kitchen with June, fixing her third cup of coffee and fuming, when Lamar sauntered through the door with a box of doughnuts in his hand, a half hour late for their meeting.

June frowned at him and picked up her mug to return to the reception desk. "My nephew, Ben, is dropping by later. He and his wife are buying their first house, and he wants to talk with you about homeowners' and mortgage insurance. When he shows up, I'll have him wait until you're done with your meeting," she told Salem.

"Thanks. I don't know how long we'll be, though."

June waved a dismissive hand. "Oh, take your time. He won't mind. It'll give us a chance to catch up on the family gossip."

Salem turned to Lamar and struggled to keep her voice calm, her expression neutral. "Our meeting was at nine o'clock, Lamar."

He shrugged. "I had to drop my car off for an oil change and ran into Thomas Williams at the Chevy dealership. He was buying one of those big SUVs for his wife…loaded with leather upholstery, GPS, and everything. Must have cost him fifty thousand. I told him I could write him up a real good policy on it. Who knew you could make that much money pulling teeth? That nigger must be selling crack out of his dental office."

Salem stared at him. Surely she hadn't just heard him use that word. Her professional demeanor slipped as her temper threatened to erupt. She clenched her teeth to keep from firing him on the spot.

"In my office, now. We have a lot of things to discuss."

She turned and stalked away, but he didn't immediately follow. She was hotter than the coffee she could hear him pouring by the time he finally appeared and slouched into the chair across from her.

"So, what's up?" He took a big bite of doughnut, dropping crumbs all over her carpet, and slurped his coffee.

"First of all, if I ever hear you use that word again, I'll fire you on the spot."

He eyed her and took another bite of doughnut. "What word?"

"The *n*-word."

He laughed. "You can't even say it. It don't mean nothing. Thomas calls himself that sometimes. That's just how we talk down here. We don't have the NAACP crawling all over us about every little thing."

"I'll immediately dismiss any employee who says it in this office or uses it in public. Just to be clear, I'm going to put a written reprimand in your personnel file specifically stating this policy. I don't want you to have any doubt that I've warned you."

He shrugged. "Whatever."

"Secondly, I want to talk to you about the Price Flooring folder. There's no workman's comp policy in it. Raeford Price called yesterday to file a claim and said he's sure his son's business was fully insured. I've checked through your other files and couldn't find it there either."

Lamar sat up. She definitely had his attention now. He chewed slowly on the last bit of doughnut and narrowed his eyes. "You went in my office? Through my files? I keep that door locked."

Salem leaned forward and met his glare. "I had a locksmith remove the lock and, yes, I went through files that are part of *my* business."

His jaw clenched, but he sat back and pretended to casually study his fingernails. "Well, I reckon I won't be able to find anything now that you've probably shuffled all my papers around."

"As I was saying, I couldn't find the policy Mr. Price called about, so I called the underwriter and they don't have a workman's comp policy listed for that company either. I find that odd, because it's one of the basic elements of commercial-insurance coverage. Mr. Price said he has a copy of the policies his son paid for. I've asked June to have him fax it over."

Lamar gave a disgusted snort. "That old man doesn't know everything. I wrote full coverage, and that's the policies Junior probably showed Raeford. But Junior's renewal check bounced.

I called him and he renewed just the policies on his office and equipment until he could afford the rest again."

"I'm also concerned about the number of cash payments you've been taking. Most businesses would write a check or use a credit card to keep a record of their business expenses."

"Well, that ain't how people do business around here. And I wasn't about to accept another check from Junior since the first one bounced."

Salem sat back. He seemed to have an answer to almost every thing, but her gut told her not to trust him. "In the future, I want to review every policy you write and I want to approve any cash payments. In the meantime, I'm going to review all of your records to see what other accounts have incomplete policies."

"The hell you will." Lamar jumped up, his face red, and pointed at her. "After your daddy got sick, I was the only one keeping this business running. He was hardly in this office for nearly a year. This business should have been mine when that old man kicked the bucket, but he left it to his queer bitch of a daughter."

"You're fired. I want you to leave immediately. Don't bother going into your office. I'll have June pack any personal items and drop them by your home."

"Your old man couldn't fire me and you can't either. I know all about the Bolander fire. You try to get rid of me and you won't have a business after you pay for the insurance fraud your old man pulled off."

"I don't know what you're talking about."

"I'll just bet you don't. You ain't been in town a month and you're already thick as thieves with Bolander's freak of a daughter. What have you girls been doing out there at her place? Stirring up her witch's pot to cast some spells? Or maybe you've been too busy licking her pussy. Yeah, I'll bet she's just like you."

"That's enough, Lamar."

Salem blinked at the uniformed police officer whose hulking figure took up most of the open doorway.

"This ain't none of your business, faggot-lover," Lamar snapped.

"I just heard Ms. Lacey tell you to leave, and I think you better do it before I pick you up by the scruff of your scrawny neck and carry you out," the officer said calmly.

"Fine," Lamar spat. "You're going to regret this, bitch. I'll open my own office. We'll just see how many God-fearing people in this town want some queer handling their insurance." He leered at Salem. "One day, a man's going to put you in your place and teach you what women are made for. Wouldn't mind doing that myself."

The officer stepped forward and grabbed Lamar by the back of his collar. "That sounded like a threat to me, Ms. Lacey. Do you want to press charges or maybe take out a restraining order?"

"No, thank you, Officer. Just get him out of here, please."

Salem sank back in her chair and closed her eyes. Her heart was pounding, and she took a few deep breaths to calm it.

"I see you met my nephew, Ben."

Salem opened her eyes to find June standing in front of her desk. "That officer is your nephew?"

"Yep. Good thing he picked this morning to stop by."

"Yes, something of a coincidence, huh?"

June smiled. "Yes, a coincidence. Just like you accidentally hitting the office intercom. We could hear everything."

Heat crawled up Salem's cheeks when she remembered the accusation Lamar had made about her and Knox. "Sorry about that. I didn't know he'd get that nasty."

"Don't worry, hon. What's said in this office stays in this office. Ben won't say anything. His best friend is gay and the godfather to Ben's oldest girl."

"Really?" Holy crap. Was Oakboro a feeder town to Key West or something? She kept finding gay people everywhere she turned. And straight people who didn't seem to have a problem with it. She wanted to laugh. Had her father realized after he moved down here that Oakboro might have a higher percentage of gay residents than Atlanta did? Ha. This was where he wanted to move to save her soul and straighten her out?

June wrinkled her forehead at the mewing sound coming from under Salem's desk. "What in the world?"

Salem smiled when a soft paw snaked out of the pet carrier at her feet to pat her leg. She picked up the carrier and set it on her desk.

"This is Tuck. He showed up at the house the day I arrived and I haven't been able to convince him to leave." She opened the door to the carrier and Tuck sauntered out, waving his tail in the air as he surveyed June. "I've got an appointment with Dr. Shepherd this morning to get his vaccinations and—"

"Oh!"

The kitten suddenly launched himself forward and dug his tiny claws into June's ample bosom to scramble up to her shoulder.

"Tuck, no. I'm sorry. He thinks he's part bird. He likes to sit on my shoulder." Salem reached for the kitten, but June put her hand out to stop her when he began to purr and rub his cheek against hers.

"What a cute little charmer," she said. "My Jimmy was allergic to animal hair, so we couldn't have pets. Since he's passed on, I've thought a few times about getting one for company."

"I've been telling her she needs a puppy to go home to." Ben had returned and grinned at them. "My wife's poodle has a new litter. I'm trying to get her to take a pup when they're ready. They don't shed much and a dog can be a lot of company."

Tuck jumped down and batted Salem's pen across the desk before pouncing on her curled phone cord and rolling around to tangle himself in it.

"Isn't that cute." June beamed.

"He's busy, that's for sure." Salem glanced at her watch, then gave Ben an apologetic look. "I'm sorry, but I have an appointment with the vet. I really appreciate your help with Lamar, but I'm afraid I'll have to reschedule a time to meet with you."

June tickled Tuck's stomach and began to unravel him from the phone cord. "You know, I've got to make a deposit at the bank. I could take the little scamp to his appointment."

"I couldn't ask you to do that." Salem hesitated, remembering what Tony had said about Doc Evan. *He needs to meet somebody, but he's such an old grump I don't know who would have him.* She looked at June. Both were widowed and needed companionship.

What could it hurt? "But if you really don't mind, I could stay and take care of Ben. Then I need to do some serious digging into Lamar's files."

June gently pushed the kitten back into his carrier and smiled. "I don't mind at all. It's Evan Shepherd's clinic out on the highway, right? Your father used to disappear once a week to go fishing with him, but I only met him once or twice."

"Yes. That's the one. Tell Doc Evan I said hi and ask how Guardian's doing."

"I'll be glad to, hon. Let me take this little fella and gather up my purse and the bank bag, and I'll be on my way."

She watched June leave and Ben grinned at Salem.

"I hear Doc Shepherd's partial to redheads."

Salem smiled back. "Hmm. Imagine that."

Chapter Fourteen

The barn's beautiful," Salem said. "When did you finish it?"

"Last week. Hoke and James helped me get everything ready and move the horses from the small barn yesterday."

"Hoke and James?"

"Hoke's been my father's groom since I was a kid."

At that moment, a tall, light-skinned African-American man led a dark gelding through the door at the other end of the long barn facility. A broad smile lit his face as he approached.

"Bonjour, Knox. Who do we have here?"

"James, this is Salem. The friend I told you would be riding with me this morning. Salem, this is Hoke's son, James."

"Pleased to meet you, James."

Instead of answering, James turned to Knox. "You didn't tell me she was so beautiful."

Knox glanced at Salem and blushed. "Cut it out."

Knox's growl didn't deter James.

"Ah, je vois. Vous vous conservez celui-ci pour vous, mon ami?"

Salem laughed. "Before you say any more, you guys should know I minored in French in college. Thank you for the compliment of accusing her of wanting to keep me for herself, James."

He exaggerated a look of surprise. "Intelligent, too."

"Are you French, or do you just speak the language to impress women?"

"I'm not French, Miss Salem, but my mama's Creole." James's European accent suddenly became a Georgia drawl. "My daddy's taken care of the Bolander Friesians since he and Mr. Robert were young men." He ran his hands down the thick neck of the black gelding. "I was always tagging along because these horses have fascinated me as far back as I can remember. When I was old enough, Mr. Robert helped me get an apprenticeship with a big farm owned by one of his friends in France. That's where I've been for the past ten years, training horses. Daddy called me a couple of months ago to tell me Mr. Robert had died and Knox had moved back to rebuild the stable. That's why I'm here."

Knox nodded. "I've got my own work to do and it's a full-time job—buying, showing, and breeding—to build the reputation of a stable. Hoke semi-retired, so I've hired James."

"That sounds wonderful. Are you riding with us today, James?"

"No, I promised my mama I'd drive her to New Orleans so she can see her sister while I visit a couple of farms over toward Baton Rouge. They have mares I want to take a look at next week. But I have your mount right here. This is Bastille, Mr. Robert's gelding. He's as gentle as an old dog."

"That's good because it's been years since I've ridden. He's beautiful."

James turned to Knox. "Who will you ride, boss lady?"

"Legacy, I think. I'll get her while you saddle Bas."

Knox led a tall mare from a nearby stall. Her wavy forelock nearly touched her nose, and her tail was so thick and long, it clearly would have dragged in the dirt if it hadn't been neatly cut off at her heels.

"Wow," Salem said.

"Bas is a more traditional Friesian. A bit stockier. My dad preferred them, but Legacy has the more modern build, taller and leaner, that's preferred in the show ring."

Salem held out her hand for the mare to sniff. "I guess I thought they were a Spanish breed because of the movie about Zorro. But you said James trained in France?"

"The breed originated in the Netherlands as a light draft horse, but they're all over Europe and the United States now." Knox checked the mare's feet for embedded stones. "They were originally bred to carry knights wearing heavy armor, but when the Spanish expanded into the Netherlands, Friesians pulled carriages there, then later became popular as plantation horses. They've been somewhat competitive as dressage horses only recently."

They led the horses outside, and Knox easily sprang into the saddle while James cupped his hands to give Salem a leg up.

"You ladies have a very nice ride," he said with a wave.

Salem appreciated that Knox started out slow. But Bas had incredibly smooth gaits and in only a short time she was urging him into a jog. Knox kept pace alongside her on the wide sandy paths that wound through the wooded areas separating open fields and a handful of small ponds.

After about an hour, they dismounted under the shade of a massive pine that stood like a tall sentry over a muddy pond. A blue heron fished on the opposite side and turtles sunned on every available rock and log. They sat in the short grass and listened to the sounds that filled the air around them. Squirrels chattered, a fish jumped, and the horses stood nearby, cropping at the grass with sharp teeth. The morning was already heating up with the promise of a sweltering afternoon, but cooler air drifted up from the pond to make it pleasant enough.

Salem purposely sat closer than she knew Knox would find comfortable, but after a little shifting about, she settled and seemed to accept Salem's intrusion.

Knox put her arms out behind her and stretched her long legs before her while Salem sat cross-legged, plucking blades of grass and taking in the oaks that lined the pond. It was more private than the irrigation ponds on the edges of fields planted with ankle-deep Bermuda hay.

She turned toward Knox and leaned back on one arm to match her pose. "Your land is beautiful. Almost as beautiful as its owner."

Knox looked away, and Salem marveled that it took so little for Knox's neck to flush red. Surely many people had told her she was beautiful, many times.

"I wanted to end the leases on these fields to turn them back into pasture," Knox said, sidestepping the compliment. "But the farmers depend on the income from the crops, so I struck a compromise. Instead of paying money to lease the fields, they pay me in hay so I don't have to buy any. One of the farmers plans to retire in two years, and I'll reclaim his fields as pasture when he does."

Salem accepted Knox's retreat. "That's really nice."

"Just trying to be fair."

Salem held Knox's gaze. "I'll bet you've always been the type to do the right thing."

Those gray eyes could be so innocently earnest one moment, then wary the next.

"Not really. My brother and I got into trouble a lot when we were kids."

"You have a brother?" As soon as Salem asked, she remembered Knox had said she didn't have any living siblings.

"He died of a heart condition right after he turned eighteen."

"I'm so sorry. You two were close?"

"A twin. He was my best friend. I'd do anything to make him laugh. He got picked on a lot, and I had kind of a short fuse when it came to people being mean to him."

"That's not a bad thing. It's understandable, Knox," Salem said softly.

"Well, I had a short temper about other things, too. That's sort of why the Institute arranged for me to work with Master Kai…so I could learn to control my…anger."

"That was where you were sent to school, right?"

"Yeah. It was like…like a Montessori school. You advanced at your own pace there. My father didn't feel the local schools here were equipped to help me reach my potential."

"How old were you when you went off to school?"

"Eight."

"Oh, Knox. That's so young. You must have been homesick."

"I missed my brother a lot, but I came home on holidays… at least, until my brother died. After that, I couldn't stand to face his empty room. My father would come to visit me once a year. It wasn't too bad. My classes were really interesting. I liked that part."

A comfortable silence hung between them as they watched the heron snatch a small fish from the water and gobble it down. Salem was heartened that Knox was sharing so much about herself. A question had been burning in her mind for the past twenty-four hours, so she decided to take a chance with this new trust between them.

"Were you here when your father's barn burned?"

Knox nodded.

"Do you remember much about it?"

"I'll never forget it…all those horses dying." Her voice was almost a whisper. "I had nightmares for years." She stared over at the horses. "I've had a few since I came back."

"God, I'm sorry. Let's talk about something else."

"No. It's okay. I don't mind discussing it with you."

"I just wondered…I had to fire Lamar yesterday."

"Lamar?"

"He's the agent who worked for Dad. He was furious and claimed that my father and yours collaborated to file a fraudulent claim. I checked the file, which listed the cause as wet hay that spontaneously ignited."

Knox sighed. "I was just a kid. I told you I used to have problems controlling my temper. It was right before I went off to school, so a lot of rumors went around that I was sent away because I started the fire. That's probably what he was talking about. I'm surprised you haven't heard it already from someone else."

Salem thought back to the women gossiping about Knox in the grocery store. How bad was her temper?

Knox's gaze was direct and penetrating. The air around them seemed to buzz. "I didn't start that fire."

Salem laid her hand on Knox's tense arm and felt a distinct, but not unpleasant, tingle run up her arm. "No, I'm sure you didn't," she said softly. "People can be so cruel." She didn't let go until she felt Knox relax. "I'm surprised you wanted to come back here."

"I have a lot of good memories, too. My father and I used to take long rides together. We'd talk about everything. He was a historian and always said history wasn't about dates and time, but about people. We'd ride for hours while he told me about the generations of Bolanders who lived on this land. Those stories made me feel so tied to this place that, in spite of everything else, it still feels like home."

"It must be amazing to have family roots that deep. Thank you for sharing that with me."

"Where's home for you? Atlanta?"

"I don't know that I think of it as home any more. That's where I grew up and my mom still lives there. She's a dance choreographer for theater productions. She loves Atlanta."

"But you don't?"

"I used to, but too much happened. I had to get out of there."

The images she'd worked so hard to banish flooded back—Eve naked on top of that woman, the media camped out at her home and workplace after she outed Eve at the funeral, and her boss's face when he fired her. She tore angrily at the grass and threw the shredded pieces away from her. She felt Knox watching her, waiting for more.

She sighed. Something inexplicable happened when Knox was near, something that warmed and steadied her. She wanted to tell her everything. Knox wouldn't repeat it all over town. She was as much of an outsider as Salem was. Besides, Knox had shared the nasty rumors about her barn fire. Salem should tell her about Eve. Tony had said her dad didn't believe you could trust someone who wasn't honest about herself. She needed to be honest. She stared down at her hands and gathered her courage.

"My lover died."

"Had you been together a long time?"

"Four years. We didn't live together, though, because she was a representative in the Georgia House and didn't want anyone to know she was gay."

She counted her heartbeats as she waited for Knox to respond to the fact that her lover was a woman.

"But you loved her?"

Not hearing any condemnation, Salem continued.

"I thought I did. We'd just gotten back from a romantic weekend in the mountains where I proposed to her. When she dropped me off at my house on Sunday night, she promised that we'd move in together after the election this fall. Then she went home and, by morning, she was dead. They said it was an undiagnosed heart defect."

"That's so awful."

"No. What was awful was finding her that morning, naked, in bed with her gardener. Apparently, she'd tied the woman to the bed and was fucking her when her heart gave out. The woman couldn't get loose. I had no idea she was seeing other people or that she was into kinky sex."

Salem's throat tightened around her hard laugh. She'd burned with anger after the funeral, but now enough time had passed that the flames of her fury had died out and only pain was left. She blinked back tears and felt Knox's long fingers curl around hers and warmth spread through her. She looked up into eyes glinting like silver and a face so beautiful, its expression so tender, she hurt in a different, wonderful way.

Knox wasn't sure who had moved, but every ounce of her was helplessly drawn to, intently focused on, Salem's mouth. It was only inches away.

"I promised myself I'd never get involved with another woman. But I'm not sure I want to keep that promise," Salem whispered, her breath a sweet feather against Knox's skin.

Something inside Knox shifted. Her head swam, heart pounded, blood pulsed, and the earth seemed to move around them. Moving. Swaying. The long needles of the huge pine fanned the thick air, and the leaves of the oaks around the pond danced. The trees. Shit!

Knox sat back and jumped to her feet. "I, uh, think there must be a storm coming."

Salem blinked. "Wha-what?" She looked up at the cloudless blue sky.

"The wind. Didn't you feel it, making the trees sway?"

"Uh…I guess."

"Oh, and I forgot that Doc Evan said I could pick up Guard today, then I need to finish some work. We better start back."

Salem got to her feet. "Okay," she said slowly. "I should go tackle some of the paperwork at my office, too."

They mounted and rode a direct route to the stable instead of the meandering one they'd taken to arrive at the pond. When they reached the barn, Knox handed the horses over to James and walked Salem quickly to her car. Knox looked at everything around them, avoiding Salem's gaze.

"Thanks for inviting me out," Salem said. "I had fun."

"Yeah, me too."

Knox shuffled her feet. Salem shifted uneasily. The comfortable familiarity between them had vanished, but the electricity crackling in the air was off the scale.

"Well, good luck with Guard."

"Thanks. Don't work too hard this afternoon."

"See you later."

"Yeah. See ya."

❖

Damn, damn, damn. She'd really screwed things up.

How could she have misread Knox so badly? Just because she didn't freak out when Salem told her about Eve didn't mean she was gay. But it was Knox who'd taken her hand and moved to kiss her, wasn't it? Had she just assumed Knox was getting ready to kiss her because she was holding her hand to comfort her? She replayed what happened in her mind. She wasn't sure.

She was sure she wanted to kiss Knox. She wanted it very badly.

Knox's rejection stung. She should be developing a thicker skin by now. Her father had rejected her. Eve had betrayed her. All of her friends, except Alisha, had dumped her. Apparently nobody loved her but her mother and Tuck. Salem mentally checked the date. Saturday. Her mom would be at the theater directing the matinee show. Well, that left Tuck to comfort her.

Instead of going straight to the office, she drove home to make herself a sandwich and pick up the little fur ball. It had never bothered her before to be alone, but she had gotten used to his company. He made her laugh at his silly kitten antics and warmed her when he curled in her lap and purred himself to sleep. He could play around the office while she worked.

Three hours later, Salem quit pretending to read the files and sat back. She'd vowed to put the morning debacle out of her mind, but Tuck had knocked a stack of files over onto the floor before she could even settle into her chair. When she bent to pick them up, the Bolander folder was the first one she touched.

That took her instantly back to the morning's ride.

Knox had a natural athletic grace, but in the saddle she seemed to become one with the tall, prancing mare. She was a Centauress, her shining black hair a perfect match to the mare's glossy, ebony coat. She was so beautiful, even the memory of Knox's shy smile stole Salem's breath.

She had to stop thinking about it. After all, how well did she really know Knox? She admitted that she had to have help managing her anger. What if a dark side lurked under that shy, innocent act? In her gut, she knew that wasn't the case. She didn't know how she knew, but she did.

As pathetic as she felt, she still wanted to get to know this incredible woman better, especially if she decided to stay in Oakboro. She frowned. When had she gone back to thinking she might stay? She shook her head at her ricocheting thoughts.

Next time she saw Knox, she'd suck it up and apologize. Clear the air. Assure Knox that she wanted to be friends. And hope Knox still wanted the same.

❖

Knox settled Guardian onto the thick dog bed in her lab, one of three nests she'd prepared for him with a water bowl nearby. The others were in rooms where she spent the rest of her time, her bedroom and the kitchen.

He was already getting around quite well with his cast. He drank from the water and sank gratefully onto the comfortable pad, his dark eyes following her as she settled at the bank of computers a few feet away.

"You going to be all right there, boy?" Though he was deaf, he seemed to sense when she was speaking to him. His tail thumped happily against the floor in response, just like it had when she showed up at Doc Evan's to bring him home. He was certainly happier than she felt after her botched morning.

She strapped on her anti-static wristbands. Christ almighty. They felt like training wheels. But this project was three-quarters done, and she couldn't risk erasing the program because a stray thought flung a burst of energy through her fingertips.

She took a deep breath and blew it out. What a geek she was. Salem was about to kiss her. She'd been dreaming about the possibility for days. Then when her lips were mere inches away and she was about to experience her first real kiss, she lost it. She was disgusted with herself.

She opened her triage-training program and copied the file that held the basic code to generate a virtual patient. She needed to create a female patient who had been in a car wreck and appeared at first glance to be fine. This patient would teach a nurse or doctor to recognize some very subtle indications of hidden injuries. She began typing away to add specific features to the file, like hair and eye color, facial and body features, to distinguish this patient from others in the program that displayed different ailments.

As she typed, her thoughts kept turning back to Salem. She'd never forget the sun picking out the blond highlights in her light-brown hair and those green eyes holding hers. She wanted to feel Salem's breath on her face again. Her mouth watered at the thought of how Salem's would taste. Crap. She would've made a fool of herself. Salem was probably an experienced kisser. One kiss from Knox and she'd know she was a beginner. How nerdy was that?

More than ever, Knox was convinced she'd never be able to have a relationship with anyone. She was kidding herself if she thought she could maintain control because all it took was Salem's smile to send her synapses popping. When Salem touched her innocently on the arm, the energy inside Knox roiled like a gathering tsunami.

She angrily typed the last string of code and hit Enter, startled when the three-dimensional image projected in front of her was a dead ringer for the woman tormenting her thoughts. The image reached up to tuck a stray strand of hair behind one ear, mirroring one of Salem's gestures. Her fingers had inadvertently typed in code that brought the woman in her head to life in her lab.

"You're as crazy as your mother, Bolander," she muttered to herself.

"Are you Dr. Bolander?" the virtual Salem asked when the name triggered a keyword and the program responded.

Knox shook her head and paused the program. If she couldn't control her energy, she'd have to find a way to explain it to Salem. If that sent her packing, then so be it. She wanted to be with Salem more fiercely than anything in her life, and if she had even a small chance, she had to risk it. She wanted to feel her body, absorb her energy. And Christ, after a lifetime of never being held, rarely being hugged, she wanted desperately for Salem to touch her… everywhere.

She drummed her fingers on the desktop and stared at her cell phone, then punched a speed-dial number and held her breath while it rang.

"Hello?"

"Hi. It's Knox."

"Hi."

"I, uh, I brought Guard home. He's much better and getting around really well with his cast." Stupid, stupid. That's not what she wanted to say.

"I'm so glad. I feel terrible about hitting him, but I'd feel worse if he didn't recover."

Okay. So small talk wasn't a bad idea. She searched for the next thing to say.

"Knox?"

"Yeah?"

"I'm sorry about today. I didn't mean to make you uncomfortable—"

"God, no. You didn't. I was calling…to apologize to you."

"Really?"

"Yeah. I'm such an idiot."

"No, you're not." She could hear the smile in Salem's voice.

"I am, too." She cleared her throat to summon her courage. "I wanted to know if you'd like to maybe go see a movie tomorrow afternoon."

"That sounds good. I'll watch most anything but horror movies."

"The theater downtown has older movies. They're showing *X-men* and *Wolverine* all weekend."

"That's superhero comic-book stuff, right?"

"Sort of, but it's not animated. If that's not your style, we can go to the multiplex out on the highway and see a new release."

"I never saw the *X-men* movies, but I loved the Xena series, and I guess it's the same kind of fantasy stuff."

"Xena?"

"You never saw that television show?"

"I don't guess I did."

"Then you, my friend, must come to my house one weekend for a Xena marathon. But for now, we'll go see your wolfie movie."

Knox was relieved at Salem's teasing tone. "Wolverine. It's an entirely different animal."

"What time tomorrow?"

Knox pulled up the movie schedule on her screen. "The afternoon movie starts at two twenty. Can I pick you up at two? It's only a few streets from your house." She was already a little nervous. This seemed more like a date than a horseback ride.

"Two sounds good." Salem paused. "Knox?"

"Yeah?"

"We need to talk about this morning, but I don't want to do it on the phone. We'll discuss it tomorrow. Okay?"

"Sure. Okay. See you tomorrow." Now she was really nervous.

Chapter Fifteen

The movie that showed at two twenty was *X-Men: The Last Stand*, a rousing fight between good and evil and an appropriate commentary on prejudice versus acceptance. But Knox had hardly noticed. All she could think about was the heat of Salem's energy gently folding around hers, the brush of Salem's hand when they reached for popcorn at the same time, and, God almighty, the vision of Salem licking the buttery remains from her fingers.

She put the Jeep in Park next to Salem's back door and they sat in silence, both fidgeting and searching for words. Guardian sat in the backseat, his tongue lolling from his mouth, watching them expectantly. He seemed to love riding in the open Jeep, so she'd brought him along for moral support. She'd parked under a shade tree and he waited patiently while they were in the movie, but he whined now and shifted on the seat. Salem reached back to pet him.

"Oh, sweetie, I'll bet you need to water the bushes, don't you? Lift him out, Knox," she said.

They watched as the dog gratefully lifted his leg and wet down the first bush he sniffed, Knox aware they were stalling and their promised talk was still ahead of them.

"I've got some spaghetti sauce in the freezer. It won't be anything fancy, but I can thaw it and cook some pasta if you can stay for dinner."

"That'd be great. I'm getting so tired of sandwiches and cereal I was contemplating trying a handful of Guard's kibble." Knox was relieved to have more time. She still hadn't figured out how to explain everything to Salem.

Salem smiled. "I think I can do better than kibble. I even have some ice cream for dessert."

Guardian limped behind them into the cheery little kitchen, only to be greeted by a tiny fur ball of spitting fury as Tuck reared up on his hind legs, needle-like claws extended and his hair standing on end to make himself look bigger than his three pounds.

The big dog pressed against Knox's legs and peeked around her at the deadly threat.

"He won't attack, will he?" Knox tensed and put her hands out to intercede should the kitten launch himself at them.

Salem laughed as she bent to scoop Tuck into her arms. "You two should see yourselves. He's tiny, and you look like you're facing down a bear. Sit down. I'll protect you from the little devil."

"I'm not sure a bear would be as scary," Knox said, cautiously taking a seat at the table and motioning for Guardian to lie on the floor next to her.

Salem soothed the ruffled cat and returned him to the floor where he sat like a little sentry between his owner and her guests. His tail twitched as he eyed his canine rival while Salem dumped the frozen sauce into a pan to warm.

"When I make spaghetti sauce, I always cook enough to freeze a dozen or so single portions. I learned that from my mom," Salem said. "We both had really busy lives, but she didn't like to feed me fast food, so she froze things we could prepare quickly or I could cook for myself when she had to run off to a theater performance."

"Can I do something?" Knox asked.

"Sure. You can help with the salad and pasta."

The delicious aroma of the sauce began to fill the kitchen as it heated.

"I tried a couple of those frozen dinners from the grocery store. They were okay, but they didn't smell this good." Knox's mouth was already watering and her stomach growling for a taste.

"Come over here and I'll show you how to boil pasta so I can send some of the frozen sauce home with you. I wouldn't want Guard to starve because you've started eating his food."

Knox signaled for Guardian to stay, figuring he must be less imposing to the cat when he was lying down. Tuck crouched, his tail still twitching, but he seemed more curious than angry now.

She followed Salem's instructions and they laughed together as they chopped salad fixings and tossed strands of pasta against the stove's splashboard to test its readiness. After Salem declared the pasta perfect, she explained that a less messy way was to just cook it for ten minutes, then taste a piece to see if it was done. Knox thought flinging it against the wall to see if it would stick was more fun.

They filled their plates and were about to sit down when Salem nudged Knox and silently tilted her head toward the animals.

Tuck crept forward and tapped his paw against the red, gauzy Vetrap covering Guardian's cast. He cautiously sniffed it and tested his claws against the hard plaster. When Guardian extended his nose and sniffed at the kitten, Tuck rubbed his cheek against the cast and Guard gave him a big lick on his small head. Tuck batted away the shepherd's nose with his tiny paw, but he purred and kept his claws sheathed. Guardian's tail thumped against the floor and Tuck skittered and hopped, playfully batting at it.

"Looks like we have a détente in the war between cats and dogs," Salem said. They shared goofy grins and settled down to their meal.

"So, how'd you like the movie?"

"It was great." Salem's eyes lit up with enthusiasm. "I love epic tales like that where good battles evil. It's also fun to pick out the social commentary."

"Social commentary?"

"Yeah. You know, like the kids at the school were gathered there because they were different. And at least one was considering taking the serum so she could be like the majority of humans, rather than a mutant."

"Uh, yeah. I see what you mean." Knox chewed her food slowly. "I used to think religion caused so many bloody wars and cruel acts because it seems to separate and alienate people, not to mention all the fanatics it attracts. But then I realized that religion was simply an excuse. Behind all of it is the human nature that balks at any horse that doesn't belong to their herd. That kind of thinking is hard to understand if you're the one being excluded." She shoveled in another mouthful and mumbled around the food. "This is really good. Much better than kibble."

"Thanks, I think." Salem sipped her iced tea. "Wouldn't it be great to have a superpower?"

"You think so?" Knox's heart picked up at Salem's reaction.

"Well, yeah. Don't you?"

Knox shrugged.

"If I had to choose, I don't know which one I'd want. I loved the boy with wings. Wouldn't it be cool to be able to fly?"

"That same boy tried to pull out his feathers when his wings first sprouted because he didn't want to be a mutant." Knox stared down at her plate and twirled the pasta around her fork. "Maybe some people really do have unusual abilities. Maybe there's a school where they hide away so other people won't hurt them or so they don't hurt other people."

Salem seemed to consider that possibility. "I love to read books about it, but I don't believe anybody can see into the future and stuff like that. I saw an old rerun of a late-night talk show where some guy supposedly could bend spoons with his mind. Turns out it was just a magician's trick."

"You think so? The laws of physics can't fully explain a lot of things."

Salem was looking around the clutter of dishes on the table. "Where'd I put the pepper?"

The condiment was out of Salem's view, behind her glass of tea, so Knox focused on the glass and it began to move.

"Whoa," Salem said, grabbing for it. "Did you see that? I need to have the foundation of this house checked. This floor must be slanted." She folded a napkin and set the glass on it. Hey, there's the pepper."

"The floor's okay. I just used my superpower to move it so you could see the pepper shaker." Knox smiled cautiously.

"Yeah, right. It's more likely that condensation ran underneath the glass and it slid on the water. Watch me use my superpowers to get the ice cream. It's called walking."

She gathered their dishes and piled them in the sink, then went to the freezer to get the ice cream. Knox concentrated again and wrapped her energy around the handle to pull the freezer door open just as Salem reached for it.

"Damn, this floor is uneven. Now the freezer isn't closing properly."

"Salem—"

"You don't mind eating out of the carton, do you? Grab two spoons out of that drawer on the left."

Salem placed the round, pint-sized container between them and reached for the spoon that Knox held out. Before her fingers could close around it, the handle wilted. Salem narrowed her eyes at Knox.

"A nerd and a magician." She snatched the other spoon from Knox's hand. "Now we're going to have to share a spoon, too."

Knox opened her mouth to say there were more in the drawer, but decided she was interested in what Salem meant by sharing. Salem dug out a spoonful and the ice cream disappeared into her mouth. "Yum. I love chocolate mint."

She scooped out another spoonful and held it out. When Knox reached for it, Salem shook her head. "Open," she said softly. Knox moved forward to take the offered treat.

Salem stuck the spoon into the ice cream and sat back. "We need to talk about yesterday and I need to tell you something."

"Okay." Knox fingered the spoon Salem had abandoned, then scooped out another mouthful for herself.

"I think…I mean…something almost happened yesterday and I think it made you…uncomfortable. I don't want you to be uncomfortable around me, Knox. You're the first friend I've made here, the only friend near my age."

"Me, too," Knox said, and held out a spoonful of ice cream. After a moment's hesitation, Salem sat forward. Knox watched in fascination as her lips closed around the spoon and the ice cream disappeared.

"Look at me."

She raised her gaze from Salem's mouth to her eyes.

"I'm gay, Knox. I'm a lesbian," she said softly.

Knox couldn't stop the heat that rose to her cheeks. "I know that."

"Do you realize how attracted I am to you?"

"No. I mean, I didn't know for sure. Tony said he could tell you liked me, and Doc Evan thought so, too."

"You guys talked about me?" Salem's tone indicated this news didn't please her.

"Salem, it's okay, 'cause, uh, you know—" She put the lid back on the forgotten ice cream so she wouldn't have to look at Salem when she said it. "Uh, I kinda like girls, too. They were ribbing me about us spending time together." There. She'd said it.

Salem returned the ice cream to the freezer and turned around to prop her back against the refrigerator. The sudden, but obvious distance Salem had put between them puzzled Knox.

"Oh, I see." Salem stared at the floor, her face red. "So it wasn't the fact that a girl almost kissed you yesterday. Having *me* almost kiss you had you running back to the barn. You should have just said you didn't feel that way. It's not like I haven't been turned down before."

Knox sprang from her chair, startling Guardian and Tuck, who'd curled up against the dog's side. "God, no. It wasn't that." She stood in front of Salem wringing her hands. She wanted to touch her so badly, to gather her in her arms. But the ruffled curtains over the sink were already stirring, and if she touched her right now she might blow every fuse in the house. "I can't imagine anyone turning you down. You're so incredibly beautiful. I wasn't uncomfortable, I…I was nervous."

Salem looked up. "I make you nervous?"

"Really nervous," Knox said weakly. "Not many women go into physics and biomedical engineering, so I usually was the only female around." She wrinkled her nose. "I wasn't interested in the guys and sort of intimidated them."

"I guess so. You were probably so much smarter than they were. Men don't like that."

That wasn't really the reason. They all knew about Knox's telekinetic tantrum that wrecked the Institute's science lab. But

Knox decided to tackle one confession at a time and she needed to stumble through this one first.

"So, well, I mostly work and ride my horses. I haven't had much time for a lot of girlfriends and other things like, um…and you're so beautiful, you must have kissed a lot of women. So, um, I guess I was afraid I'd disappoint you." It was a miserable, mumbling finish, but she'd managed to choke it out.

Salem's soothing energy flowed around her like a blanket for two heartbeats before she felt the warm hands on her cheeks. Salem's gaze was soft. Her lips were silk. Knox closed her eyes and gave herself over to it, following and mimicking the caress of Salem's mouth against hers.

Salem spun them around so that Knox's back was pressed against the icebox. Her mouth was insistent against Knox's, her tongue begging for entrance. Knox opened to it and tasted the warm chocolate mint. She thrilled at Salem's body pressing against hers. When Salem's nipples hardened against her breasts, her last threads of control disappeared. Energy rolled through her like a firestorm and burst forth. Salem moaned as she absorbed the brunt of it, and the fluorescent bulb of the overhead light fixture shattered. They sagged against each other, panting.

"Wow," Salem breathed. "Now that's what I call a kiss."

Knox grinned and hugged Salem to her. "When the contractor comes to check out the slanted floor, maybe you should have him look at the wiring, too."

Chapter Sixteen

"Dr. Bolander, a car has entered the front gate and is approaching the house." The smooth feminine voice of the security system filled the lab where Knox bent over a keyboard, absorbed in the code she was typing.

"Identify."

"Sensors show a 2010 BMW 335 convertible, color red, custom Georgia plate LACEY, Fulton County. Heat scan indicates a driver, no passengers. Would you like a retina scan to verify the driver?"

"No! Um, no. Stand down. This is an approved visitor."

"Should I log that as a permanent approval?"

"Affirmative. Full access."

Knox typed furiously to finish the code, then sprang from her chair. She ignored the elevator and slid down the banister of the stairway, jumping to the landing below and hopping onto the next banister to descend from the third level to the first in record time. As soon as her feet hit the foyer floor, she wished she'd given herself time to think this out. Even though she and Salem had parted with a heated kiss two days before and talked on the phone several times since, Knox had a sudden attack of nerves. Greet her with a kiss, a hug, a smile? A car door slammed. No time to ponder.

She yanked the door open just as Salem lifted a wicker picnic basket from the backseat and turned to smile at her.

"Hey, you. I know you said you were working on a deadline, but you have to stop every once in a while to eat." She held up the basket. “Gina, at the diner, recommended the country fried steak and peach cobbler.”

“Sounds great. I’m starving.” It really wouldn’t have mattered if Salem had brought dirt for dinner. The surprise visit thrilled Knox. She took the basket and received a peck on the lips as Salem swept past her into the foyer. Knox felt about ten feet tall.

“Dr. Bolander, will you be returning to the lab soon, or would you like me to save and close your open programs?”

Salem raised her eyebrow at the disembodied voice.

“That’s DIVA, my assistant.”

“Diva?”

“Detect, identify, verify, and authorize. A security system I designed.”

A loud woof sounded at the top of the stairs.

“Your canine requires assistance, Dr. Bolander.”

Salem laughed. “If she can do housework, too, I may want to test her at my house.”

Knox grinned. “Unfortunately, I’m currently designing virtual, not robotic, assistants.” She glanced at the stairway. “Right now, I need to take the elevator to bring Guard down here. He can’t manage the stairs with that cast on his leg.”

“Awaiting response, Dr. Bolander.”

“Stand by.”

“Can I come up with you? I’d love to see what you’re working on. That is, if it’s not something top secret.”

“It’s not. I’m working on a medical-triage program.”

Guardian greeted them when the elevator opened onto the third floor and thumped along behind as they entered the lab.

“The program provides a series of scenarios where doctors in training have to react under pressure.” She sat down and began typing. “The scene I’m working on now teaches a new doctor to multitask in a disaster situation. The doctor will encounter a virtual patient that requires immediate surgical attention. Once he’s immersed in the procedure to remedy that problem, another virtual nurse appears and describes a different patient’s emergency condition for evaluation. Her report is sketchy, so the doctor must ask the correct questions, without pausing work on the first patient, to adequately evaluate the second patient."

Knox stopped typing and dropped her head to her chest, her eyes closed.

"Is something wrong?"

"You're going to think I'm a perv."

Salem chuckled. "What did you do?"

Knox hit the Enter key and held up the virtual surgery gloves. "I might as well show you. Put these on. You're not squeamish, are you?"

"Uh, maybe. Why don't you wear them and I'll watch?"

Knox slid a headset that looked similar to wrap-around sunglasses over Salem's eyes and grabbed a second headset for herself before leading her over to the metal table.

"Initiate program."

Salem jumped as a surgical team appeared around them and a patient materialized on the table, gasping for breath. Virtual scrub nurses undressed the patient as Knox grabbed a virtual stethoscope and put it to the man's chest.

"No respiration on the left side." She held out her hand to a virtual scrub nurse. "Chest tube."

Salem jumped at the sound of it slapping into Knox's hand. "Wow. This is so realistic."

The virtual team didn't respond, but Knox smiled as she slid the tube between the patient's ribs.

"Doctor, we need you immediately in treatment-room three."

Another nurse, dressed in maroon scrubs, appeared on the other side of the table, and Salem gasped. She felt like she was looking in a mirror.

"Freeze program." Knox blushed and fumbled with the gloves as she took them off. Her cheeks heated as Salem stared at her doppelganger. When Knox had changed the features on the triage patient that resembled her, she missed virtual Salem. So she recreated her as a trauma nurse.

Salem walked around the table and circled the nurse.

"I…I didn't intend to leave her like that. I mean, I wasn't going to put your face in medical schools all over the country. I meant to change it before I released the program. I've totally freaked you out, right?" She threw the gloves on the table. "End program. I'll change it now."

Salem caught her hands and smiled shyly up at her. "I think you're incredibly sweet."

"Yeah?" The knot in her stomach began to relax. "So you don't think I'm a pervert?"

"She doesn't strip out of those scrubs for you, does she?"

"NO. God, no." The very thought mortified Knox.

"Then you definitely aren't a pervert. You are, however, in bad need of glasses. She's much prettier than I am."

Knox smiled. "No way. Virtual Salem doesn't hold a candle to the real thing."

"Sweet talker. I can't believe some woman hasn't snatched you up before now."

The heat spread from her cheeks to her ears under Salem's affectionate gaze. God, she wanted to kiss her, but she didn't want to come off like a teenaged boy, pawing at her.

"How 'bout we go dig into our dinner before it gets cold?" Salem said.

Knox wasn't sure if she was relieved or disappointed that Salem had redirected the moment. "Just let me close these programs."

While she shut down her computers, Salem stared at the empty table where a life-like virtual patient had been fighting for life just moments before. "You know, creating people out of computer code is sort of like a superpower."

"Nah. It's really not all that complicated."

"Ha. I'll bet you have some sexy tights and cape hidden around here somewhere. Virtual Woman to the rescue."

Knox laughed. "With that imagination you should write novels, not sell insurance." But the mention of superpowers reminded Knox that she did still have a secret to reveal. So, when they stepped into the elevator, she used her energy to press the button for the first floor.

Salem didn't seem to notice. She was busy scratching Guardian's ears and giving him kisses on his long nose. They retrieved the picnic basket they had left in the foyer.

"How about we eat on the terrace and take an evening ride?" Knox offered, telekinetically opening doors and turning on lights as they walked through the house. But Salem just chattered away about her day, as though a house with automatic doors and lights was nothing unusual.

"I'd love that, but are you sure you have time? I don't want to keep you from your work."

"Virtual Woman is a bit ahead of schedule, so I've got time." It was only a small lie, but she'd work all night if she could spend the evening with Salem.

The nearly full moon illuminated the sandy paths in soft light, and the pines fanned their needles gently in the breeze as they walked their horses at a leisurely pace. They talked about everything and nothing. What's your favorite thing to do on a rainy day? What do you like to read? If you had one year to live, what would be on your to-do list? Do you believe in God? Democrat or Republican? They didn't talk about their families or what had brought each of them back to Oakboro.

The sultry night and the company were so perfect, Salem didn't want her Eve disaster to intrude. But she did want to pinch herself. Knox was just too good to be true.

She was intelligent and engaging when she relaxed. When she was nervous…well, Salem found Knox's shyness over her inexperience completely adorable.

Her eyes glinting silver in the moonlight and her dark hair loose about her shoulders, she was a vision of strength and beauty. She sat the saddle like a royal guard, escorting her queen to some unknown castle.

But even beyond that, Salem felt something when she was around Knox…a warmth that infused her, made her feel safe. And when Knox touched her, every nerve in Salem's body tingled.

They ended up by the river and dismounted.

"Sit here," Knox said, indicating a thick log that had obviously been cut and placed in the grassy clearing as a bench. They settled side by side and Knox whistled softly. "Be very still and watch."

After a moment, a pair of snowy white swans silently glided into view. They circled, suspicious of the newcomers, but made straight for the shore when Knox pulled a small bag from her pocket and began tossing out bits of crusty bread. They watched the swans gobble up the bread until it was all gone. When the swans realized the meal was done, they curiously eyed the strangers, then returned to the water, grumbling in little grunts, then swam a slow, circuitous route back to their nest on the opposite shore.

"They're beautiful."

"They're a mated pair my father found here about twelve years ago. Don't know where they came from. They're certainly not native to the area, but he began feeding them to get them to stay. Said he liked to come out here to watch them and think."

"They mate for life, don't they?"

"Mostly. My father believed in that. My mother, well, she isn't easy to live with. She's a high-functioning autistic."

Salem tried to remember what little she knew about autism. She had, of course, seen *Rain Man* with Tom Cruise and Dustin Hoffman. And a really interesting BBC documentary on the autistic woman, Temple Grandin, who designed some type of device to treat herself and then used it to calm cattle in slaughterhouses.

"I don't know much about autism," she said. "Just that they like to keep a routine and are sensitive to touch and sounds."

Knox nodded. "It was my responsibility to keep my brother quiet when she was around."

"I thought you were the same age."

"We were. But he was mentally handicapped." Knox shrugged. "My mother claimed that I stole his brain cells when we were in the womb together. I know it's medically impossible, but I didn't know that when I was a kid. Even when I was old enough to know that wasn't true, I still felt responsible for him."

"That must have been hard."

"Yeah, I guess. I really didn't mind. My mother didn't like to be touched very much, so we pretty much got our physical comfort from each other."

Salem reached for Knox's hand and folded it in both of hers. She marveled at the tingle that ran up her arms and the goose bumps that instantly appeared. "I guess that explains why, when I first met you, it seemed like you had a really big do-not-cross line around you. It seemed like you jumped every time I touched you," she said softly.

Knox stared at their joined hands. "I don't mind when you touch me now. I…I like it when you kiss me."

That was all the invitation Salem needed. She had to know if what she felt last time was just a "first kiss" phenomenon.

Their lips met in a brush and Salem slid her hand behind Knox's neck to draw her closer. She marveled at the taste of Knox's tongue against hers, the current that flowed through every part of her body and sparked a steady throb between her legs.

Did she crawl into Knox's lap, or did Knox move her there? Her head was swimming. She could swear the trees, the leaves were dancing around them. They tumbled backward into the grass and Knox's long frame trembled under her. Damn, she could come just from kissing this woman. That would be embarrassing.

"Stop. We've got to stop." Salem pushed up with her arms only to realize that she was pressing her hips into Knox's pelvis. She rolled off and they lay on their backs next to each other, breathing hard.

"What? Why? Did…did I do something wrong?"

Salem turned on her side. Knox's eyes were a thundercloud.

"God, no. I had to stop before…I don't usually jump a woman just for kissing me. I seem to lose all control around you."

"Yeah. I know what you mean."

She could see the relief on Knox's face before she scrambled to her feet and offered her hand to help Salem up.

The ride seemed too short on their way back, but she knew she'd taken up more of Knox's time than she should have. She expected to find James in the barn because the lights flicked on as they approached, but nobody seemed to be around as they unsaddled the horses and brushed them down.

"Do you have motion sensors in every room, or does DIVA do that?"

"The lights? Uh, no." Knox put Salem's horse in its stall and slid the door shut. "Actually, uh, that's kind of my superpower."

"Superpower?"

"Yeah. I'm telekinetic, what you call a spoon-bender."

Salem laughed. "Virtual Woman may have a secret power, darlin', but it's not bending spoons. It's being able to render women senseless with a kiss. Your lips should be registered as a lethal weapon." She didn't want to think about what else Knox could do with that mouth, or she'd never leave. And she really had to let her get back to work. "I hope I haven't made you miss the deadline on your contract."

"Nah. I do my best work late at night." Knox put her horse away, too, and turned to her as the lights blinked off and darkness folded around them like a cloak. Knox pulled her close and kissed her until Salem thought her knees would buckle.

"Very slick," Salem murmured. "Eventually, I'm going to figure out how you do that."

"I told you. It's my superpower."

"If you say so." Salem stepped back, but held tight to Knox's hand, reluctant to break their connection. "It's time for me to go home and for you to get back to work."

Knox sighed. "If I have to."

Doors swung open and lights flicked on in each room as they walked through the house. Salem didn't bother to gather up the picnic basket, because she was afraid if she lingered she wouldn't have the fortitude to leave.

Clinging to her last shred of willpower, she keyed the electronic locks on the BMW as they cleared the front door. If she could just get in her car, then Knox couldn't press that hot, sexy body against her when they kissed good night and maybe, just maybe, she had a chance of sticking to the plan.

But her finger, or possibly her resolve, must have slipped because the locks clicked back into place and then she was again in Knox's embrace, surrendering to a mind-melting kiss.

"God, you're dangerous," she gasped, holding Knox at arm's length. "If you don't stop, we're going to end up naked in the backseat of this car." The locks disengaged again with a click. Everything, even her brain, seemed to short-circuit around Knox. Salem climbed into the car and lowered the window.

"Come back for lunch tomorrow," Knox said, squatting to put herself at Salem's level.

"I can't tomorrow. I have a state insurance auditor coming in the morning. Why don't you drive into town? I'm sure I can get away long enough for something quick at the diner."

"One o'clock, at your office?"

"One is fine." She smiled and caressed Knox's cheek. "Now let me go while I have a few brain cells still functioning."

Knox's gaze held her prisoner a moment longer. "Good night, Salem."

Chapter Seventeen

The diner was still hopping just after one. Every table and all but one stool at the counter was filled, so they stood in the doorway and debated going to a chain restaurant out on the highway.

"Hey! Y'all here for lunch?" Gina expertly balanced six plates on her arms as she paused on her way to a table.

"I don't have much time," Salem said, "and it looks like you're all full up. Maybe we'll just take something back to my office to eat."

"Nonsense. Some of these people need to get up out of my chairs and go back to work anyway. Give me half a minute."

"Really. Takeout is okay," Knox said quickly.

"I won't hear of it." Gina distributed the plates of food and walked over to a group of men lingering in a booth. "Time for you boys to clear out. You know Joe's gonna be mad if y'all are late getting back from lunch again."

One man grinned up at her. "Joe's gone to Valdosta for some car parts. He ain't gonna know how long we took for lunch."

"He's gonna know when I complain next time he's in here that you boys took up a table for a whole hour when I could be seating someone else and earning another tip."

"How 'bout we add a dollar to our tip for you to keep quiet and bring us some more tea?"

"Why, Hank Briley, you big spender. Added to your usual, that'd be a whole dollar fifty. I reckon I can finally take my mama to Hawaii."

The other men laughed and Hank turned red.

"Go on, now, I got customers waiting. Just tell Jimmy what y'all had and he'll ring it up. Tell him I said to throw in a couple iced teas to go."

The men grumbled but obediently slid out of the booth and headed for the register by the front door where Knox and Salem waited. Gina waved over a teenager with a dishpan and he began to efficiently clean off the table.

Knox shifted uncomfortably. She wasn't used to being in crowds. Salem seemed to sense her uneasiness and squeezed her hand.

Hank looked at their joined hands and snorted. "Can't believe she's kicking us out to give our table to a couple of lezzies," he grumbled.

The other men turned to them to see who he was talking about, but Doc pushed through the door at the same moment.

"Well, well. Didn't I get lucky…two of my favorite ladies," he said.

Hank snorted again and Doc turned to stare him down. "Y'all running late, aren't you, Hank? I just rode past Joe's shop and saw Mrs. Jefferson waiting out front, tapping her foot because the lunch sign was still up."

"Shit. All I need is the boss's wife breathing down my neck." He threw his money on the counter. "Give the change to Gina, Jimmy. I gotta run."

Jimmy rang up the meal and shook his head at Hank's departing back. "She should throw him out more often. He left a whole eighty-eight cents this time."

Gina swept past with a tea pitcher and held out her hand for the tip. "Every little bit helps, I reckon." She indicated the clean booth with a jerk of her chin. "You ladies have a seat. I'll be back in a minute to take your order. Doc, you want to sit at the counter? That's all that's available right now."

"He can sit with us. Right, Salem?" Knox was relieved for the reinforcements. Hank's rude comment gnawed at the lining of her empty stomach.

"Sure, that'd be great." Salem glanced after Hank. "Stupid redneck," she muttered under her breath.

Doc waved a dismissive hand in Hank's direction but ran his gaze over the parking lot. "Well, now, I'm expecting some lunch company myself." He smiled. "But if she doesn't mind eating lunch with her boss, we'd be happy to join you."

Knox was surprised. "You're having lunch with June?"

Doc looked at Salem. "That okay with you?"

Salem grinned. "That's wonderful. We'd love for you guys to sit with us."

They had barely sat down when June arrived. She laughed at being found out but was happy to share her lunch date with Salem and Knox. They could all relax, she told them, because the auditor had announced that he was taking a two-hour break.

Knox and Salem decided to share a cheeseburger plate so they could save room for the day's special dessert, fresh apple pie à la mode. June ordered a chef salad, explaining that she was trying to shed a few pounds.

"You're fine just the way you are," Doc said. "I don't know why women want to be skinny. I like a woman with a little meat on her bones."

June winked at the girls. "He's such a sweet talker," she said, causing Doc to blush. She patted his hand. "It's a good thing, Evan, if you plan to keep company with me. I'll never be thin. I just want to be able to stay in the size I'm wearing now, and that requires turning down a few pieces of pie every now and then."

Knox began to relax as the lunch conversation flowed around her. Salem bragged about Knox's virtual projects, and June announced that Doc had talked her into taking one of the pups from her nephew's poodle.

"If you don't mind the silly haircuts, poodles are smart dogs. Ben and Susan's female is good-tempered and has solid bloodlines," Doc said. "How's Guard doing, Knox?"

"He's great. It was too hot for him to wait in the Jeep, even with the top down, so I left him at the barn with Hoke." Knox stifled a yawn as she finished off her dessert. "Sorry. I was up late, working."

"What time did you finally go to bed?" Salem asked.

"Uh, haven't yet."

Salem huffed. "I can't believe you're sitting here eating lunch after working all night. You could have called. I'd have understood."

Knox shrugged. "I work through the night sometimes when I get in a good groove. It's not a big deal. I'll catch a nap this afternoon." Nothing would have kept her from an opportunity to see Salem. "Besides, I wouldn't want to miss out on this apple pie…or the company."

Doc chuckled. "Now who's the sweet talker?"

"Well, well, well. Who do we have here?" Lamar sauntered over and leered at Salem and Knox. "The bitch and the freak, a perfect couple."

"Nobody's interested in anything you have to say, Lamar, so why don't you go sit down."

"That's not exactly true, Doc. I hear there's an auditor at Franklin's office right now, digging into the books. I'll bet he's interested in what I have to say."

Salem narrowed her eyes. "I asked the state insurance commission to send the auditor after I got a look at the mess in your office."

"I'm not stupid. You've got nothing on me. I made sure of that." Lamar sneered. "But I've got the goods on your daddy and the freak's daddy there for filing a false claim. When that auditor's done, you'll be lucky if they don't shut down your daddy's office and put the freak in jail for starting that fire and lying about it."

"You don't know what you're talking about, Lamar. You'd be wise to shut up before you incriminate yourself," Salem said.

"Franklin Lacey ran an honest business and you know it." June scolded him. "Your poor mother, I don't know what she did to deserve a child like you. She told Franklin you were trouble, but he was determined that you'd straighten out if he gave you a chance."

"If that old man wanted to straighten somebody out, he should have started with his queer daughter. Get it? Straighten her out." He laughed loudly and the diner grew quiet as his voice carried across the room.

Knox had heard enough. She was exhausted and her control was stretched paper-thin. Lamar was the same bully who had constantly taunted her brother, Ham, on the elementary-school playground. When she stood, she was several inches taller than Lamar. She put her face close to his, her voice low and cold.

"You want to pick on someone, pick on me. But you better not open your mouth about Salem again. You hear me? If you think I kicked your ass when we were kids, you don't want to know what I can do to you now that I'm all grown up."

She could see the fear in his eyes but, like a scared dog, he took one more bite.

"Go ahead, freak. Nobody believed me before, but they will when you do it here. You'll find yourself right back in the same nut house they sent you to after the fire. You think your lezzie girlfriend will come see you there?"

The empty table next to Lamar began to vibrate. She was about to snap. She had to get out of there. She was losing it. Too emotional, too embarrassed to even look at Salem, Knox threw a twenty on the table and stalked out the door.

"Freak," Lamar yelled at her retreating back.

Salem wanted to slap him but she was more concerned about Knox. She slid out of the booth to follow, but Doc's hand on her arm stopped her.

"She'll be fine," he said. "I've known her since she was a kid. She needs to be alone when she's angry. Give her some space. She'll cool off and get some sleep and be fine by tomorrow."

Salem didn't believe that. It might have been the only option Knox ever had before, but she didn't have to cope with things alone anymore.

"Salem, honey, you're supposed to be meeting with the auditor in fifteen minutes," June said, her voice full of sympathy.

Damn it. Standing him up wasn't an option. Maybe she could answer his questions quickly, then go find Knox.

❖

"Salem, it's six thirty. Do you need me to stay? I can."

She looked up from where she sat on the floor with insurance contracts spread all around her. Dan Atkins, the auditor, was sitting at Lamar's desk, working through a different stack of contracts.

"No, you go ahead, June. Aren't you supposed to meet Doc Evan and pick out your puppy tonight?"

"If you need me here, I can phone Ben and tell him I'll come by tomorrow instead."

"Dan?"

"No, she can go. I'm about to call it a night, too, after I get through these two files."

"All righty then. I'll let Evan know I'm headed that way."

Salem was relieved. She was finding it hard to concentrate on a bunch of boring contracts when all she could think about was finding Knox.

In spite of her preoccupation with the lunch incident, she found some clear irregularities with the accounts. She looked up when Dan slapped the last file closed.

"Something's not right here, is it?"

"You were definitely smart to request an audit. The first red flag is the amount of cash business this office handles, all of it collected personally by Lamar. I'm sure you know that's unusual in the insurance business. Also, I'm seeing a pattern of full coverage on new contracts, then some portions of the accounts being dropped upon renewal. The items selected for non-renewal are always areas that have a low incidence of claims."

"That's not unusual in an economic downturn. If a client came to me and said he couldn't afford his policy any longer, I'd advise him to drop some of the coverage that rarely warrants a claim. I'd rather do that than lose the client."

"And you'd be right. In these cases, however, the coverage being dropped doesn't significantly reduce the price of the individual policies to benefit the client, and nearly ninety percent of the accounts Lamar maintained were slightly reduced. Collectively, the difference in premiums amounts to a tidy sum."

"You think he was skimming."

"That's my suspicion, but we need more than a hunch to file charges or pull his license. Even though I'll have to finish my audit and file a report, I can pretty much predict that an agent will be assigned to investigate both your father's and Lamar's personal finances. In fact, I'll be making a call tonight to have those accounts frozen immediately to prevent any transfer of assets until the investigation is complete. That could take thirty to sixty days. I'm sorry."

"It's no problem. I can live off my savings for a while. But this office writes policies for over half the town's residents and businesses. I'd like to request that the state appoint a financial trustee during the investigation so we can continue to collect premiums and write new policies."

Dan scribbled in his notebook. "You seem to know a lot about insurance investigations."

"I worked as a regional manager for a number of years in the commercial division of a large insurance firm based in Atlanta. We had a few occasions to request audits on a branch office or two, so I'm familiar with the process."

"That'll make things easier and perhaps expedite the investigation. I can make some phone calls first thing tomorrow to arrange for a trustee." He clicked his briefcase closed. "But right now, I plan to find some place to eat dinner before they roll up the streets around here."

Salem smiled. "Then you better hurry. About the only place still serving after nine p.m. is the Lock'n Load tavern, and I've been told you'd never eat there if you got within smelling distance of their cook."

"Thanks for the advice."

CHAPTER EIGHTEEN

When Salem rang the doorbell, she heard the locks disengage. Maybe Knox was working in her lab and had released them from there. She walked inside, but the foyer was dark.

She jumped when a voice sounded behind her. "Welcome, Ms. Lacey. Dr. Bolander is not currently in the residence. Would you like to wait?"

That security system was creepy, like having an invisible person in the walls.

"Guess it lets everyone in the house," she said to no one.

"Retina scan indicates you are Salem Lacey, age 32, owner of a 2010 BMW 335 convertible, color red, custom Georgia plate LACEY, Fulton County. Dr. Bolander has authorized for you to have full access to the estate. Background security check belayed."

Salem chuckled. "You sound a little jealous, Diva. Can you locate Dr. Bolander for me?"

"Dr. Bolander was last detected in the main barn."

"Thank you."

But Knox wasn't in the barn and Bas was gone. Salem sat on a hay bale to wait and started thinking about the fire twenty years ago. Knox had lost so much: her home, her family, the horses she loved. Sweet, beautiful Knox.

Deep in thought, she was startled when light suddenly flooded the barn's interior and pushed back the twilight that had settled around her.

Knox, grim-faced and silent, rode past without acknowledging her. The tense set of her back as she dismounted and unsaddled the gelding told Salem everything and nothing.

"Knox," she said softly.

Knox put the saddle away in the tack room and began to brush the horse with short, rough strokes. "What are you doing here, Salem?"

"You left without saying good-bye. So, I came as soon as I could get away from the auditor to make sure you're okay."

She heard no response but the sound of the brush stroking the gelding's hide.

"Have *I* done something? Are you angry at me?"

"No."

Salem took a deep breath and grabbed Knox's wrist to stop her. "Then tell me what's wrong."

Knox turned her face away, so Salem gently grasped her chin and turned it back. Still, Knox wouldn't meet her gaze. She could feel the walls, big thick barriers, but she knew in her heart that Knox didn't really want to be alone any more.

"Knox, baby, tell me what's wrong. That stupid Lamar isn't worth this, no matter what information he claims to have."

Knox jerked away from Salem's grip and began brushing again. "You shouldn't get mixed up with me."

"I'm already involved with you. Wait. What exactly does Lamar know that I don't?" Had Knox lied when she said she didn't start the fire? Salem tried to remember her exact words.

Knox's hands stilled and she stared at the ground. "He knows I'm a freak."

"Surely you don't believe that. It's just childhood jealousy. Being incredibly smart doesn't make you a freak. You're adult enough to know that."

Knox closed her eyes and took a deep breath, as though gathering herself, then turned back to Salem.

"What I'm going to tell you isn't a joke, Salem. I'm being completely serious. Do you understand?"

Salem nodded.

"If you repeat it to anyone except Doc Evan, who already knows, I'll have to go away. Forever. I'll have to leave my home and my horses again."

"I'd never do anything to hurt you like that. I care about you too much."

She held Knox's gaze, willing her to trust, begging to be let inside the walls that Salem was learning had protected, imprisoned Knox since she was a child.

The expression on Knox's handsome face, however, wasn't acceptance. It was a challenge: *Hurt me. I know you will. Hurt me now before this goes any further.*

"When I was only a baby, they discovered that I was… different," Knox said. "At first, when I was an infant, the curtains rustled when I cried to be changed or fed. When I was a toddler, my parents would find me playing with things that had been placed out of my reach. They had no idea how I was able get them. Then one day, when Ham and I were two, we were sitting at the table, eating cookies. Ham wanted another, but my mother said no because it was too close to dinner. I wanted another cookie, too. So I put out my hand and the plate of cookies slid within my reach. I'm telekinetic. I can make things move by manipulating the energy around them."

The skeptic in Salem was having a hard time accepting what Knox was saying.

"You can move things without touching them?"

"I guess you want a demonstration." Knox sighed. "Just don't freak out on me, okay?"

"I won't. I promise."

Salem's keys lay on the hay bale where she'd been sitting. Knox put her hand out, and after a few seconds, the keys levitated and moved through the air to rest in her palm.

Holy shit! The possibilities raced through Salem's head. Was this some sort of weird dream? That was it. She'd fallen asleep on the hay bale and this was a dream.

Salem felt Knox watching her and, when she looked up, she could see on her face that Knox expected rejection, revulsion. She could *feel* her bitter disappointment. *Okay. This is Knox, shy genius and lover of all animals. Pick your words carefully.*

"Lamar knows about this and that's why he calls you a freak?"

"I had trouble controlling it when I was younger. The kids at school picked on Ham a lot because he was slow. When I got really angry at them, things would fly though the air, kids would fall down, stuff like that. Lamar was the worst bully on the playground, and one day I just lost it with him. No one else was around and I wanted to scare him enough that he'd leave Ham alone. I levitated him almost to the ceiling and he peed his pants. Ham told all the other kids. They, of course, didn't believe the part about me lifting him to the ceiling, but one of the other kids saw Lamar leaving school in his wet pants."

Salem chuckled. "No wonder he hates you. But I'm sure he only got what he deserved."

"That wasn't how my parents saw it when Ham told them. The Institute wasn't just a school for really smart kids, Salem. My father had a friend who worked there. He promised they could teach me control."

"So that's why your parents sent you away when you were only eight?"

"Yeah. Mostly." Knox seemed to collapse in on herself. She dropped onto the hay bale and covered her face with her hands. "So now you know. I really am a freak."

Salem sat next to her and wrapped her arms around her hunched shoulders. "Oh, baby, I'm so sorry. I can't imagine how lonely you must have been, taken from your family, from your brother when you were still a child. But you definitely are not a freak. Unusual, maybe. Extraordinary, for sure. But not a freak."

Knox trembled, and Salem didn't understand how she knew, but the walls began disintegrating, vaporizing. It wasn't her imagination. She *was* feeling Knox's energy, her emotions coil through her every time they touched. Could Knox feel her?

"You really don't think I'm a freak of nature?" The lonely child isolated by her gift, not the accomplished adult, asked the question.

Salem squatted in front of Knox and caressed her cheek. "No, baby. You're the most beautiful, talented woman I've ever met. Maybe an honest-to-God superhero. Not to mention, the best damn kisser in the world."

"Yeah?"

The hope, the tentative exultation that radiated from Knox made Salem want to cry. "I could use a reminder," she whispered.

Knox's mouth was so sweet on hers. A warmth flowed around them like the gentle lap of water against a dock, but Salem wanted more. She wanted the electricity that usually surged through her body when Knox touched her.

She deepened the kiss, sliding her tongue into Knox's mouth and rising to straddle her lap. Knox slipped her hands under Salem's shirt, and a tingle skittered along her spine and raced outward. Salem whimpered. Her nipples and clitoris pulsed with a pleasure so sharp, she ground her crotch against Knox's taut belly and moaned. She found Knox's breasts and rubbed her palms over them. Her nipples were hard under the thin material of her shirt, and Salem rolled them in her fingers.

The barn's lights began to flicker and the horses moved restlessly in their stalls.

"Stop," Knox gasped, pulling away. "We have to stop."

"What?" Salem's head was hazy with desire. "What's wrong? Knox?"

Knox stood and set Salem on her feet at arm's length. "I have to stop."

Salem suddenly felt foolish. Christ, she was seconds away from orgasm, just from kissing this woman. "I'm sorry. I didn't mean to attack you like that, but you do something to me that makes me forget myself." She pressed her hands to her chest, trying to settle the fluttering of her heart.

"God, Salem, I can't think at all when you kiss me like that." Knox's hands shook as she ran her fingers through her hair. "You make me feel, I don't know, out of control."

Relieved, Salem laughed. She grabbed Knox's hands and held them in hers, marveling at how the energy still rolling off Knox raised the hairs on her arms. "Is that so bad?"

"You don't understand. I really want to…with you, but I can't. I can't do this. Things can happen when I lose control."

"What things, baby?"

"I don't know. Bad things." Knox stared at the floor and shifted nervously, like she'd bolt if Salem released her hands.

"Bad things have happened before?"

Knox nodded and tried to pull her hands free, but Salem tightened her grip. She didn't know what their future might hold, but she wanted to help Knox face whatever demons made her believe she had to spend her life alone.

"Knox, honey, look at me." She waited while Knox fought whatever battle was going on inside. When she finally looked up, her heart tore at the desolation in Knox's eyes. "Tell me, baby. Tell me what you're afraid will happen. Has someone been hurt before, when you didn't stay in control?"

"Yes. No. Almost."

"Tell me what happened."

"There was a girl at the Institute, a year older than me. I wanted to spend every minute with her and began to have thoughts that went beyond friendship. I thought she felt the same. But one day, I walked into the science lab and she was kissing a boy, one of our classmates, and I lost it."

Knox closed her eyes against the memory, still stark and sharp.

Glass beakers exploded and test tubes flew across the room to crash against the wall. Bottles and instruments were swept from the tables and cabinets onto the floor where the chemicals spilled from their containers and mixed to give off a noxious cloud that swirled around her. She gasped for breath. The last thing she remembered was clutching her throat and calling for Ryan. But Ryan didn't come.

"Things started flying around the room. Anything glass shattered. Chemicals spilled everywhere. I couldn't breathe. I blacked out and woke up two days later in a hospital room with Master Kai sitting by my bed. He had been assigned to teach me how to keep control of my energy and not wreck things."

"Was your friend or the boy hurt?"

"No. They crawled under a desk. I never saw them again. They were transferred to another school."

"How old were you?"

"About thirteen."

As Knox gripped Salem's hands, Salem wondered what it must have cost that thirteen-year-old to lose still another person she'd trusted with her feelings.

"We're talking about two very different emotions here. Passion, not anger, is happening between us. You're telling me about an adolescent tantrum. She was your first crush. Did something happen the first time you slept with somebody, too?"

Knox ducked her head and didn't answer.

"Knox?"

"She was my only girlfriend," she mumbled.

Salem's heart jumped. Had she heard wrong or were all the women where Knox had been living completely blind? Knox was gorgeous, smart, and sexy beyond reason.

"You're telling me that you've never—?"

Knox's ears reddened and she nodded. She briefly glanced up at Salem. "You remember the first day we met and the light bulbs in the chandelier exploded? It was when you touched my arm. I…it had been so long since somebody actually touched me. So you can see why I was afraid of what could happen if I got really excited."

"When you were at my house and the kitchen lights shattered while we were kissing?"

"You were kind of blowing *my* fuses."

Salem smiled, pleased with herself, and Knox finally smiled back. She cupped Knox's face in her hands and kissed her thoroughly and with purpose, savoring the softness of her lips, the taste of her mouth, and, most important, the quiver of Knox's body. When the lights began to flicker again, she ended the kiss and rubbed her thumb across Knox's lips.

"Just for the record, I'm not afraid of your gift, and I'm not worried about a few broken light bulbs. But we'll go slow if you're afraid." She gave Knox a quick peck. "Now, what else do you need to do out here?"

While they were putting away things in the barn, Salem's phone signaled a text message. Dan had appointments to interview several clients with suspicious files first thing in the morning and wanted Salem to accompany him. Ordinarily, the agency under investigation wouldn't be allowed at the interviews, but Salem had requested the audit and the suspicious activity took place before she assumed ownership. She typed back that she would meet him at eight o'clock, and she and Knox strolled under the moonlight, arm in arm, to her car.

After a long good-bye of searching kisses and murmured apologies, Salem had to end their evening. She put her hand on the car door, surprised that the lock engaged.

Knox grinned. "I did that on purpose."

"Well, Dr. Bolander, as much as I'd like to stay and test your control, even superheroes don't get everything they want. As punishment for this little display of mischief, I need to leave you with a little homework." She waggled her finger in Knox's face. "But if you blow my headlights, I'll be driving your Jeep home."

She whirled them around to press Knox against the car and hold her there as she claimed her mouth in a heated kiss. Slipping her thigh between Knox's, she thrust slowly. Knox's jeans were damp, her crotch hot. Her low moan turned to a high-pitched whimper when Salem found her breasts again. With one last soft brush of their lips, Salem stepped back.

Knox sagged weakly against the car, her chest heaving and her eyes so hungry Salem wanted to say "screw work" and drag her to the bedroom. But she needed to let this pot simmer.

"Your homework, gorgeous, is to go climb in bed," she took Knox's right hand and swiped her tongue slowly against the long fingers, "slide these fingers between those long, sexy legs, and think about that kiss…without shattering the bedroom lights."

Chapter Nineteen

Knox punched the "one" on her cell phone and waited while it speed-dialed Salem.

"Hold on," Salem said. Then Knox heard a muffled, "I'll take this in my office."

After some bumping and footsteps, she heard a door close.

"Hey, baby. What's up?"

"Nothing." *I'm just missing you like crazy.* "I just thought I'd see how things are going." *I needed to hear your voice.*

"The deeper we dig, the more we're uncovering. I have no idea how this'll end up. The agency could be held liable for a lot of it. The records we're finding are unbelievable and we still have hundreds to go through. But you know I can't talk about the details. How are things with you?"

"Saving the same old virtual lives."

Knox didn't want to talk about work. It had been four days since she'd confessed her telekinetic abilities to Salem. Four days since Salem told her it didn't make a difference in their relationship. Four days since Salem had left her with a kiss that had her waking up every night from erotic dreams. Four days since Salem had time for anything more than phone calls.

"How's Guard doing?"

"Fine." *Better than me.* "He's got a new, smaller cast that lets him put some weight on that leg."

"That's wonderful."

Frustrated, Knox struggled with what to say next. In her work, she voiced keywords or typed code to make what she wanted happen. With her horses, she gave them the right cues and they changed gaits, turned, or stopped in response. She had no idea how to express to Salem that she needed to see her, to touch her, to hold her.

But Salem seemed to understand and dropped her voice to a sexy timbre. "How's your homework coming?"

Knox closed her eyes and smiled. "Not too well. I'm running out of light bulbs. I need some help from my instructor. I was hoping you could come out here for dinner tonight."

"I'm so sorry, honey. We've got more interviews tonight with people who can't meet with us during office hours."

"'S okay. Maybe another time." Knox hated that she sounded so pitiful.

"I miss you," Salem said softly. "It's just bad timing right now. You believe me, don't you?"

"Yeah…Salem?"

"What, sweetie?"

"Are you sitting behind the desk in your office?"

"Yes."

"What are you wearing?"

Salem laughed. "What would you say if I told you that listening to your sexy voice has my skirt hiked up to my waist and my hand between my legs?"

Knox nearly choked at the vision. But that was fantasy, not reality. "Well, that has me sweating, but it's not what I was asking. Describe the clothes you're wearing."

"Oh." She could hear the confusion in Salem's response. "My blue suit and the light-blue camisole I had on the day we first met. Minus the mud splatters, of course."

"Is your jacket on or off? And describe how you're sitting."

"On, of course, since I only have the camisole under it. I'm sitting back in my chair with my legs crossed."

Knox pictured Salem in her mind. She could see the office, the desk, Salem reclining with the cell phone held to her ear. She could see the blue jacket and buttons along its front.

"Oh." Salem's lilting laugh made her grin. "You're one nasty girl. Where are you? I can't believe you can unbutton my jacket all the way from your house."

Actually, Knox wasn't sure she could, either. But she could see it in her mind and apparently make it happen, even from miles away. She imagined releasing the buttons one by one, then moving her hand over one silk-covered breast.

"Oh! Knox, stop it." Salem was breathless. "Good Lord, I can feel you. You've got to stop. I don't want our first time to be over the phone, and if you keep this up, it will, at least on my end."

"Really? You can feel my hand on your—"

"I'm at work, for God's sake. Dan's in the room right next to this one."

That was a bucket of cold water. Knox didn't want to think about Dan and Salem huddled together in the office, riding together in the car to interviews, grabbing meals together while they worked. She wanted to be the one sharing Salem's days, not some guy.

"I'm sorry. I'll stop."

"Oh, baby. This won't be forever. I just can't get this business up and running and hire another agent to help me until this is all cleared up."

"I know. It's okay." Knox's words didn't sound convincing even to herself.

"If it's not too late, I'll try to drop by for a few minutes when we get done tonight."

"Sure. I'll be here."

❖

But Salem didn't stop by that night or the next three. She was dead tired, and it was nearly eleven o'clock Thursday night when she returned home to an indignant kitten.

"I know, I know. I've been a terrible mommy and an even worse girlfriend." She filled Tuck's bowl with kibble, but he ignored it and walked into the other room, tail swishing angrily.

Salem sighed. She wouldn't be surprised if she got the same response from Knox. She'd called every day to see if Salem was free for lunch or dinner. But as she and Dan dug deeper into the records and turned up more violations, Salem had to decline Knox's invitation each time.

They had to review every policy Lamar had ever written or renewed over the past five years and interview the policyholders with inexplicable gaps in their coverage. They'd also spent hours at the local bank, trying to match the agency's deposit records against scattered payment receipts they'd been able to retrieve from Lamar's clients.

Salem rubbed her tired eyes and flopped across her bed. This audit was taking much longer than they expected.

That's why Dan had been pushing hard to work through the past weekend and every evening since. Salem couldn't blame him for wanting to wrap things up so he could return home to his wife and children.

Still, Knox's trust was so fragile and their relationship so new. She hadn't called today. Maybe she was getting tired of having her invitations turned down. This was the worst possible time to be stuck in the middle of this tangled mess.

Salem was too tired for anything more than a kiss, but she wouldn't mind crawling into bed and sleeping snuggled in Knox's arms. Maybe then she'd dream of something other than insurance contracts and mismatched receipts.

She smiled to herself. Would Knox come over if she called? She said she often worked late into the night.

Salem closed her eyes. She'd rest, take a quick shower, and call Knox to invite her for a sleepover. That's what she'd do, right after she rested for just a few minutes.

❖

Salem groaned and twisted her neck to the right.

The shower and the phone call to Knox had never happened. When the phone woke her that morning, she was still lying on her back across the bed, fully clothed. Dan was calling because he'd been waiting more than thirty minutes for her to arrive and open the office to resume work. Her anticipated long, hot shower was a five-minute splash in her dash for the door.

He gave her a sympathetic look. "I'm really sorry, Salem. I feel responsible for your stiff neck. I'm sure you've got other things to be doing, but I promised my ten-year-old I'd be home in time for her big swim meet. If you'd ever had to look into her big brown eyes when she says, 'Please, Daddy,' you'd understand completely."

Salem chuckled and rubbed at her neck. "I'm sure."

"I'll bet you had your father twisted around your little finger, too."

She shrugged. "Yeah, I guess I did when I was young. But after I became a teenager, I was closer to my mom. So I stayed with her when they divorced."

"That must have been tough for your dad."

"I wouldn't know about that. All I know is how tough it was on my mother."

It was hard to be sympathetic toward her father. Even more, she was bothered by her father's culpability in the discrepancies they were finding. It would have been very hard for Lamar to commit such widespread fraud without Franklin being suspicious. Was he that lax in running his business? Was he in cahoots with Lamar? Or, like Lamar had insinuated in the diner, did he keep quiet because Lamar was blackmailing him?

The Bolander fire claim had been fraud, Lamar said. But Salem had looked at the file and it appeared to be in order. The cause of the fire was ruled to have been the spontaneous combustion of green hay, baled on the Bolander estate. Franklin and Doc Evan had also given sworn statements that Robert had expressed concern that when the hay was baled, it hadn't dried sufficiently. He'd intended to have it moved out of the main barn before the heat rose in the center of the tightly bundled bales and the nitrogen-rich hay ignited.

But that kind of fire was rare. Sure, it was a gamble every time a farmer mowed hay fields and prayed for two or three days without rain to let it dry before baling. But Salem had checked weather records for that year. That area had been in a serious drought.

She knew Knox didn't like to talk about the fire, but she needed more information. She couldn't afford to let Lamar blindside her. He was stupid to think anything that happened then could indict either her or Knox, but it could damage her business and the Bolander reputation.

She rubbed her neck again.

"Here, let me see if I can help. My wife says I'm a very competent neck masseur."

His large hands began to work her tight shoulder and neck muscles, and she moaned.

"God, Dan, that feels so good. You should insure those hands for a million dollars."

"I've heard that before…uh, hi."

The massage stopped, and Salem opened her eyes to see Knox standing in the doorway.

"Knox, hey. I was just thinking about you." If the look on Knox's face hadn't clued her something was wrong, the stillness would have. When Knox was close, the atmosphere always seemed full of electricity. Now, she was standing four feet away and Salem felt nothing but dead, empty air.

Knox set the bag she held in a chair by the door. "I brought over some lunch, but I can see you're busy. I'll just leave it here for you."

Before Salem could respond, she turned and disappeared.

"Knox, wait." Salem grabbed the bag and caught up to Knox at the front door. "Let's go in my office and eat lunch together."

"Thanks, but it looks like you've got company for lunch already. I wouldn't want to intrude."

"Stop it. I meant just you and me. Dan can get his own lunch." She grabbed Knox's hand and ignored her flinch. "Please? I don't blame you for being irritated with me. I should have put my foot down and made time for us this week. It might not seem like it, but I missed you like crazy."

Knox hesitated, and Salem tugged her down the hall to the privacy of her office where she closed the door, put the lunch bag down, and wrapped her arms around her stiff frame.

"I'm not going to let go, Knox Bolander, until you hug me back."

Knox slowly relaxed a little, then responded with a loose hug. It wasn't the greeting she hoped for, but it had taken a week to build the wall between them and it'd take more than one hug to tear it down again.

She released Knox and led her to the couch, where they sat next to each other.

"I was planning to call you last night to invite you for a sleepover, but I made the mistake of lying across the bed for just a moment and fell asleep." Salem opened their lunch. "I woke up this morning still in the clothes I wore to the office yesterday and with a bad crick in my neck. Dan was just trying to help me with that because he felt bad I've had to spend so much time in the office this week."

Knox scowled. "He had his hands on you."

Salem cupped Knox's face. "Honey, he has a wife and two kids at home. We've been working every evening and last weekend because he's anxious to get back to them." She kissed Knox softly. "And I'm anxious to get this cleared up so we can spend some uninterrupted time together."

"A sleepover?"

Salem could feel the wall begin to weaken and kissed her again with more purpose. "I was too tired for anything but a kiss, but I'd hoped that if I used you as a pillow, I'd dream about something other than endless paperwork."

Those gray eyes darkened again, but this time in a good way, and a bit of that familiar tingle leaked out from behind Knox's defenses.

The conversation still lacked their usual ease and flirty exchanges, but they talked about Guardian and Tuck, a stallion Knox favored to breed her mares, and June's new poodle puppy that seemed to have very bad health since Doc Evan's truck was parked at her house almost every evening around supper time.

"Speaking of Doc Evan, was he there the day your father's stable burned down?"

Knox picked at her food. "I don't remember. It was a long time ago."

"I know you don't like to talk about it, but I need to know what happened."

"I didn't start the fire, Salem."

"I believe that. But Lamar has made accusations that something other than spontaneous combustion started it. I can't tell you about this audit, but I can tell you that Lamar has some explaining to do. And I'm afraid he'll bring up something about that old claim to deal his way out of the pickle he's in."

"Everything you need to know is in the file."

"The fact that you won't look me in the eye tells me it isn't all in the file. Your father's signature is on a sworn affidavit, right alongside my father's."

Knox stood and paced the room, her voice louder with each step. "I was only eight years old, and I've spent every day since then trying to forget."

"Holding it inside all this time hasn't made it any less painful, has it? Maybe you should talk about it. Just tell me what you do remember."

"No!" The burst of energy that blasted out with Knox's shout toppled Salem's desk lamp with a crash.

After a knock, Dan's voice filtered through the door. "Everything okay in there, Salem?"

"It's fine, Dan. I just accidentally knocked over the lamp on my desk."

"Okay. I'll be in Lamar's office if you need me."

She waited until they heard his footsteps retreat. God, she was tired and her patience was stretched as thin as gossamer. She turned back to Knox.

"Look at me," she told Knox. "Look me in the eye and tell me everything written in the file is completely true and accurate, to the best of your knowledge. I know you won't lie. If you say it's the truth, then I'll defend it against Lamar's lies no matter what it may cost."

A tortured mix of hurt and anger flashed through Knox's eyes before her stare turned flat and emotionless. "I came here today because I wanted to have lunch with someone I cared about. I didn't know it would be an interrogation."

"You didn't answer my—"

Knox was gone. Salem jogged down the hall to catch up, but the front door slammed shut and the deadbolt clicked into place. She closed her eyes and sagged against the door. She needed a key to open it, and Knox would be long gone before she had time to run back to her desk and get it from her drawer.

"Damn you, Knox."

Chapter Twenty

Salem aimed and threw another pencil, eraser first, across the room, where it thumped against the window and fell. Tuck skittered over to bat it across the hardwood floor to a pile he was accumulating in the corner.

She told June she'd brought the kitten to work with her because, with the long hours she'd been working, he was lonely. But she'd really brought him because she was lonely.

It was Monday, late afternoon. Seventy-eight hours and forty-five minutes since Knox had stormed out of the office. Each time Salem tried to call, it went straight to voice mail. She'd promised herself that as soon as Dan left that morning, she'd drive to the Bolander estate and confront her, like she had when Knox retreated before.

So why, hours after Dan was gone, was she still sitting in her office, throwing pencils at the window?

She opened her Internet browser, searched for dartboards, and ordered one to be delivered. Hmm. Maybe she should order a punching bag while she was at it. She could hang it in the corner for when she was really pissed.

She was pissed now.

Knox hadn't lied to her, but she sure as hell was keeping a secret. Come to think of it, Eve didn't exactly lie, either. Salem had never specifically asked if she was seeing anyone else. But when Eve professed to love her, she took for granted that theirs was an exclusive relationship. And, damn it, Eve constantly implied that it was.

Knox might not be a slick politician, but she was capable of deceit. Hadn't she concealed her telekinetic abilities from the Institute? Salem was sure she was hiding the real cause of the stable fire. She could be keeping other secrets, too. That was the last thing Salem needed. Hadn't she learned her lesson with Eve?

She was contemplating whether she should raid Tuck's pencil stash so she could throw some more when June rushed into her office.

"The old Sears building's on fire. Leave Tuck here and let's go watch."

"Wait. We don't insure that building any more."

"Sugar, I don't care if it's one of ours or not. This is the most exciting thing you'll see in this town in the next five years. Now, come on. What else do you have to do?"

She had a point. Besides, they did insure the buildings on either side of the old department store, so if the fire jumped it could affect her business.

They hurried along the six blocks to the fire scene, careful to stay on the sidewalk as several fire trucks from surrounding communities joined the Oakboro department to fight the huge blaze and wet down the adjacent buildings.

Even a block away, they could feel the intense heat and see the flames shooting out from the roof. The cacophony of sirens and shouted orders was deafening.

Word traveled fast as the county's volunteer firefighters arrived one by one and reported in to join the battle. Salem was surprised when one volunteer turned and waved. It was Max.

"You be careful," June shouted over the noise.

"Always am," Max said, before trotting over to the captain to get her assignment.

The ladies' auxiliary to the fire department began to set up a rest area for the firefighters rotating off the front lines.

"Isn't that one of Franklin's buildings?" somebody asked.

The people standing near them turned to hear Salem's answer.

"It was," Salem said, "but I dropped him two weeks ago when he wanted me to match an offer Lamar made to insure it."

Everyone nodded their approval.

"Your daddy was a good man, but you may be a better businessman," one man said.

"A lot better looking, too," someone piped up from behind her.

That brought nods all around again and Salem smiled her thanks.

They watched for more than an hour, until the roof collapsed into the third floor and it was clear the neighboring buildings would survive.

June was helping set out folding metal chairs someone had brought from a nearby church so the spectators could sit along the sidewalk and continue to watch. Gina was selling egg-salad and tuna sandwiches out of a basket to the spectators who were settling in.

But Salem's fatigue weighed too heavy to continue standing there.

"I'm heading out," she told June. "Don't expect me in the office tomorrow. I need a day off."

June patted her arm. "Don't worry about it. If anything comes up that I can't handle, I'll call you."

Salem doubted there was anything June couldn't handle. And she didn't trust anyone more. Maybe she should talk to her about taking the licensing exam instead of hiring another agent.

When she walked away from the noise and bright flames, dusk had begun to quietly settle over the town. The streets were mostly empty, except for a few stragglers going to watch the fire.

The excitement of everything melted away as she neared the office and the melancholy she'd left there found her again. She retrieved Tuck and drove the few blocks to her house.

She had no appetite for dinner, so she poured a bowl of kitten kibble for Tuck and a glass of wine for herself and settled into a chair on the back deck.

Salem wondered, for the hundredth time, why she was in Oakboro and debated whether she would stay. She thought she'd found her answer when she first kissed Knox. But now she wasn't sure.

A movement at the edge of the woods drew her attention to the rise where she'd seen a horse and rider before. She stood and squinted, willing her eyes to see farther. She was right. They were there again, silhouetted against the darkening sky.

"Knox," she whispered. She started to shout and wave, but the rider descended the knoll and disappeared into the woods.

She swallowed her disappointment with the rest of her wine and went inside. Maybe a nice long soak in a hot bath would make her feel better.

But it didn't.

Five hours later she was still tossing and turning.

Was it a coincidence that Knox was lurking around town when the fire started? Twice, she'd seen her struggle for control when her anger flared. Had her temper gotten the better of her this time? Could Knox be responsible for today's fire? Had she lied about starting the stable fire all those years ago?

Salem felt in her heart that Knox could be nothing but honest.

Still, she was keeping something secret. Eve kept secrets.

She punched her pillow into a new lump and tossed around the bed, unable to find that magic position that would lull her to sleep.

What if someone else saw Knox riding on the outskirts of town tonight? Could she be arrested for suspicion? Salem had terrible visions of a small-town lynch mob and a courtroom where attorneys dressed in seersucker suits convinced slack-jawed jurors that Knox was a witch with an arsonist bent.

She sat up and threw the bedcovers back. It might be three in morning, but it was ridiculous to keep trying to sleep. She found her clothes and pulled them on.

She needed to see Knox. She needed to trust Knox. But more than anything, she desperately wanted to hold her.

CHAPTER TWENTY-ONE

Knox lay like a lump on her bed, staring at the ceiling.

She'd expected her funk to wear off after a few days. Instead, she seemed to sink deeper. She couldn't work, couldn't eat, couldn't sleep. She rode her horses relentlessly, saddling one after another, in an effort to find solace on the sandy trails of the estate. But she couldn't.

She missed her father. She missed her brother. And, damn it all, she missed Salem so badly it tore at her.

But, like everybody else, Salem wanted something from her. She wanted information about the fire, and Knox couldn't give it to her. She'd promised silence and had never intended, never wanted to break the vow…until now.

Christ. How was she going to get through this?

Guardian whined next to her bed. Her depression was affecting him, too. He wasn't eating either. When she had begun to feel light-headed earlier that day, she'd downed a couple of protein drinks and he, too, broke his fast with a bowl of dog chow. They were a pathetic duo.

God, she needed to sleep. But every time she closed her eyes she saw the fire in the old Sears building. Watching the flames from the outskirts of town had brought to life too many bad memories.

She considered drinking her way through her father's wine cellar. If she was unconscious, maybe she wouldn't hurt so badly. She'd never allowed herself to be drunk or drugged because she was afraid of losing control. She was still afraid. She closed her eyes and began the meditation steps Master Kai had taught her, but it was no use. Finally, she gave in and let her mind open up what her heart needed most. Memories of Salem.

❖

When Salem pulled up to the entrance of the Bolander estate, the gate didn't swing open as it always had. Was DIVA locked down for the night? Or had Knox removed Salem's security access? She thought about turning around. No. She'd driven out here in the middle of the night and, damn it, she intended to see Knox.

She bumped her car up against the gate and climbed on the hood to drag herself up and over the top. She dropped to the other side and jogged up the long drive.

❖

Knox's mind held tight to images of Salem when exhaustion won out, and she finally slipped into a restless sleep.

Salem was sitting in her living room, trying to drink that very sour lemonade the first day they met. Then they were riding together, the huge oaks waving their Spanish-moss-draped branches in obeisance to Salem's beauty. They were lounging in the grass next to the pond, laughing and talking and trading kisses. She could hear Salem's heart beat when she laid her cheek against her breast.

But the beating began to grow loud and discordant. There were shouts, and they were no longer at the pond. They were standing with the crowd, watching the old department store burn. Knox covered her ears to block out the sound of the fireman's axe battering against a metal door.

She turned to Salem...where was Salem? Inside, she's inside, someone yelled. No. She had to save her.

She could smell hair and skin burning. She could hear the firemen's shouts as she raced into the unbearable heat. Salem,

Salem, where are you? She saw a shirtsleeve and began tossing away bales of burning hay to reach it.

She realized the firemen's shouts had turned to terrified whinnies. Hooves drummed against the barn walls. Her hands were burning, her lungs were on fire. Ham, Ham, where are you?

She heard a sharp noise, like gunshots, and looked up. It must be the beams cracking. The roof was falling. She had to hurry, but when she looked down the shirtsleeve was gone.

Too late. She was too late.

"No!" Knox jolted awake. Gasping for breath, she sat up. She was in her bedroom, not a burning building. Sweat tricked down her back and a warm tongue lapped at it. The gunshot sound, she realized, had been Guardian's sharp bark. He pushed at her with his nose, ran to the bedroom door, and barked again. As the haze of Knox's nightmare began to clear, she realized she could still hear the banging sound from her dream. Someone was pounding on the front door.

"DIVA."

"Intruder alert. Police have been notified an intruder has breeched the main gate."

"Can you identify?"

"White female. Age 32. Five feet, five inches tall. Identified. Salem Lacey. Licensed insurance agent. Resides at—"

"Enough. Notify police to stand down."

"Notifying police."

Knox slipped into shorts and a T-shirt and followed Guardian down the stairs.

The pounding was persistent.

"God damn it, Knox. I'm not going away until you let me in and we talk. Open this door now. I know you can hear me. "

She disengaged the lock and opened it. Salem's energy hit her like a sledgehammer and she swayed weakly against its force.

"Oh, my God. Baby, are you sick? You're pale as a ghost. Come sit down."

She let Salem lead her to the sitting room where she sank gratefully onto the sofa and closed her eyes. Salem's cool hands were everywhere, checking her pulse, feeling her forehead, holding firmly to her hand.

"I knew I should have driven out here, instead of letting you stew. You could die out here by yourself and nobody would know."

"DIVA can detect any dangerous changes in my temperature or heart rate."

"DIVA is a damned computer, Knox. I know you're upset with me, but I care about you too much to let a bunch of computer chips be responsible for your health. When you're sick, you need a human to take care of you, make you soup, rub your back."

"I'm not sick," she said weakly. "I just haven't been eating or sleeping much."

Salem's aura stilled and then flowed around Knox to wrap her in a protective cocoon.

"Aw, honey, me either."

Knox opened her eyes. "Have *you* been sick?" If something happened to Salem, would someone call and let her know?

"Sick with worry. You haven't been taking my calls." Salem frowned. "Eve kept secrets, Knox. Secrets that hurt me. I'm scared because you keep secrets, too. And I'm upset that you don't trust me."

The secret Knox had held tight for so many years, the truth she'd guarded, had been her bond to the two people she loved most. But she'd have to let it go, let them go, if she wanted to hold onto Salem.

"I don't want to keep secrets…not from you." She hunched forward, clutching at the fear gnawing inside her belly. "It's just…the fire…it brings back so much."

"Baby, you're shaking." Salem wiped at the tears Knox just now realized were wetting her cheeks.

"Nightmare. When you knocked, I was having a dream about that building burning in town this afternoon. I guess then…it triggered my old nightmare about the barn. Only it was you, not Ham, I was trying to save." Her chest jerked with a sob and she struggled to hold in the years of pain that clawed to be free.

Salem's arms closed around her. "It's okay, sweetie. You don't have to tell me if it hurts too much. But you don't have to hold it in, either. You're safe with me."

Knox burrowed her face against Salem's breasts. She did feel safe here. She didn't have to stay in control with Salem. Another sob escaped and Salem's hands moved along her back in soothing strokes.

"The hay…it was high in nitrogen, but not from rain. Dad had used a new fertilizer to raise the protein level. That didn't start the fire, but he said it's what made it burn so hot and spread so fast."

Flashes of that day jolted through her, Ham grinning at her as he threw down another lit match.

"Ham was at the age when boys start to test things. Only he didn't have the mental capacity to recognize danger. He found a can of lighter fluid and was standing in the barn, squirting it across the dirt, then dropping a match on it to watch the fire crawl along the trail of fluid."

Another flash. Ham holding the can out of Knox's reach and laughing.

"I told him to stop and tried to take the can from him, but he jerked it away, spraying fluid across the barn onto some bales of hay that had been dropped down from the loft to be put in the stalls that night."

Watch, Knox. This is so cool.

Ham, no!

"He struck a match and threw it down on the floor before I could stop him. I grabbed a horse blanket and tried to smother it, but the hay bales started exploding. Ham's sleeve was on fire. I could smell my hair burning. It was so hot I couldn't breathe. The horses were screaming."

Her throat tightened so much she could hardly choke out the rest. Tears streamed down her face and soaked Salem's shirt.

"Dad ran in and yelled at me to get Ham out while he and Hoke tried to free the horses. It was hard because Ham was wailing for Dad and fighting me the whole way. There was a big 'whoosh' and the barn looked like an inferno. I was screaming, too. Then Hoke stumbled out, pulling Dad with him. You couldn't hear the horses any more, just the fire consuming everything."

Salem's arms tightened around her. "Oh, Knox. I can't imagine how awful that must have been. I'm glad all the people got out, though."

Salem's fingers combing through her hair, her hands stroking along her back gentled away the nightmare. The rhythmic thump of Salem's heart replaced the fire roaring in Knox's ears.

"It's not unusual for children to start fires. Why didn't you and your father tell the truth back then?"

"There had been several incidents before that. Hamilton was big for his age and had given another boy a black eye. He also swiped Dad's hunting knife one day and took it to school to show off, and the teacher freaked out. And he was starting to refuse to do what the teachers told him to, testing them. The guidance counselor thought Ham was becoming dangerous as he grew older and stronger, and said we should send him off to a 'special' school. She meant he should be institutionalized."

"So, you told them *you* started the fire?"

"No. Dad knew it was Ham. But he'd already talked to a friend of his about enrolling me at the Institute. The schools here just didn't have the resources to challenge me. I was only eight, but my I.Q. was off the scale." She dried the last of her tears on Salem's shirt and realized it felt good to finally be free of her secret. "Dad knew most people wouldn't believe the wet-hay story, so we agreed that I would go away immediately to make them think it was me and I was being sent to some kind of juvenile facility. Ham was tutored at home after that to keep him out of trouble."

"Oh, baby. It doesn't matter how smart you were, you were still an eight-year-old little girl. How could your parents do that to you?"

"I wanted to protect Ham as much as they did. I was scared and lonely without Dad and Ham. But when I thought of my brother, frightened and alone like that in some mental facility, I knew I was doing the right thing."

She closed her eyes and felt the tendrils of Salem's energy curl around her. Other than with Master Kai, the only time she'd sensed another's aura was when he had introduced her to another young telekinetic. His power had clashed, battled with hers, but Salem's energy had entwined and danced.

Tonight, that energy was quiet and soothing until Knox slipped her hand under Salem's shirt. The current changed then. A buzz of arousal tingled through her fingertips as she stroked Salem's smooth belly.

Her doubts fled. Salem couldn't have betrayed her with Dan. Salem's aura didn't lie. Salem wanted her. And she wanted Salem.

"Knox, honey, it's really late. Actually, really early in the morning." Salem shifted under her. "Do you think you can sleep now? You must be exhausted."

"Do you have to go?"

Salem hesitated. "You want me to stay?"

"Yes." The electricity that flowed from Salem cascaded through her, and Knox wanted more. She licked the pulse throbbing in Salem's neck. "But I'm not tired."

"O-okay."

Knox grinned and sucked her ear lobe. When Salem shivered, Knox withdrew and searched her hazy gaze. "*Is* it okay?"

"God, yes."

The consent had barely left her lips when Knox covered Salem's mouth with hers and slid her tongue inside. She wanted, had been wanting, this. She straddled Salem's thigh and rubbed against her. God, she was soaked. Going slow was a bad idea. She was way past simmer already. She needed to make love with Salem or *she* would spontaneously combust one night with her own hand between her legs and Salem in her dreams. She was ready to let go of her fears. This time, she wouldn't stop.

"Knox, stop." Salem pushed at her. "Baby, we have to stop."

"Huh?" Her brain couldn't seem to translate the word into meaning. "What? Why?"

Salem pointed at the huge glass chandelier that hung only twelve feet away. "Too much glass."

"Oh." Comprehension kicked in. "Oh-h-h."

"I want to make love to you without worrying about exploding light fixtures."

"Bedroom." Knox jumped up from the sofa and dragged Salem with her.

Every few feet Knox stopped to kiss Salem, her confidence growing, her clit throbbing with each little whimper from Salem's throat. At last, they reached the bedroom. Their combined energy swirled and snapped around them, and Knox's body pulsed with the urgency of it.

But Salem hesitated. "Your lab, your work. Is it safe?"

"Yes. I've made sure."

"Good, because I don't want you to hold back anything." Salem's chest was flushed as she peeled off her shirt, her breasts taut. She dropped her bra to the floor. "You make me feel wonderful things, incredible things. I want all of it. All of you, baby." She lowered her jeans and panties to the floor and kicked them away. "I'm not afraid and I don't want you to be either."

Knox's heart soared. She'd been waiting all her life for that invitation. For the permission to give herself completely, to take what she so desperately needed. She held Salem's gaze and slowly shed her clothes, baring herself to another for the first time. Since she'd been old enough to be aware of it, others had only pressed her to hide, to control her gift. Now, the hunger in Salem's eyes made her swell with power and she let it flow.

Salem opened her arms and spread her aura like an angel's wings, then closed around Knox, drawing their naked bodies together. She was a lightning rod to Knox's storm, a superconductor to her heat. Salem's kiss was hot and deep and urgent.

Knox had never felt another woman's skin on hers, never touched another woman's bare breasts, never tasted another woman. And she wanted it all now, every inch of Salem...with her hands and her mouth. She wanted it so badly, she couldn't think. She lowered Salem to the bed and pushed her hips between Salem's legs.

"I need you close," Salem gasped.

Knox moaned as Salem arched up to meet her, hot and slick against her belly.

Salem guided Knox's mouth to her breasts and encouraged her to explore. Knox was cautious at first, lest she hurt Salem in her frenzy of desire. But Salem would have none of it.

"Harder, baby. Suck it. Use your teeth. Oh, God. Yes, like that."

Salem undulated against her and Knox instinctively thrust back until Salem, panting, dragged her up for another heated kiss.

Salem's hand found hers and moved it to the soft curls between her legs. Even as Knox marveled at the wetness she found, she knew she was equally ready. She slid her fingers over the stiffening clit and triumphed at the jerk of Salem's hips.

"Oh, oh, baby. I'm not gonna last. Inside. I need you inside."

Knox entered slowly and hot muscles gripped her fingers. Salem's heels pressed against the backs of her thighs, guiding her like a rider would her mount, setting their rhythm, urging her thrusts harder, deeper.

Salem's energy pulled and hers answered, gathering and flowing to her own swollen clit. Knox gasped as the current surged and exploded through her. Salem cried out and Knox's body convulsed through the long soul-deep melding. The pounding of her heart—or maybe it was Salem's—seemed to fill the room as they, at last, lay together in a sweat-slicked tangle.

Salem's synapses snapped with the residual sparks of Knox's power. Even though she should be weak as a kitten after an orgasm that nearly blew out every nerve in her body, she felt energized. She nudged Knox onto her back and hovered over her, surprised to see her eyes closed and her cheeks wet with tears.

"Oh, baby. Are you all right?" She wiped at the tears and kissed Knox's slack lips.

"I can't move. You completely drained me." But when Knox opened her eyes, they shone with wonder and her mouth curved into a smile. "I think you're the dangerous one."

"Oh, yeah?" Salem licked at the salty sweat on Knox's neck. "You have no idea. But I'm willing to give you another hint."

She kissed and sucked her way down Knox's neck to her small, firm breasts. Knox had a beautiful body, long and lean and athletic. Salem licked and rolled the hard nipples between her lips, finding the pressure that Knox responded to best.

Knox's power, indeed, felt somewhat diminished, but the tingle in Salem's lips as she kissed a path along Knox's ribs signaled it was gathering again. Knox squirmed when Salem tongued her navel, and her breath hitched as Salem moved lower to the dark, saturated curls.

She nipped the inside of Knox's thigh and shouldered her legs apart. She could feel Knox holding her breath and decided not to tease. She didn't want her to pass out before experiencing the most intimate, most erotic connection to another woman possible. She nuzzled into the curls and spread her hands over Knox's belly to hold her down as she began with a broad swipe of her tongue. Knox was still hard, so she avoided the sensitive clit as she licked away the evidence of their first coupling.

Knox's moans grew louder and her hips bucked harder as Salem ran her tongue closer to its purpose. And when she pulled the turgid tissue into her mouth and sucked hard, Knox gripped the sheets and cried out as her body bowed upward in climax.

Salem smiled with satisfaction. The air seemed to pulse slowly around her, and she sensed it was the waves of Knox's receding orgasm. She crawled up Knox's limp body and kissed her, sharing the taste of her passion.

"Dangerous enough for you?"

"Criminally dangerous. You're amazing." Knox's voice was faint, her words sluggish. It had been a tense week and an exhausting day. Salem rolled over on her back and cuddled Knox against her breast.

"Sleep now, baby. No more bad dreams. I'll be here when you wake up."

Chapter Twenty-two

Salem surfaced from a deep sleep to the arousing sensation of soft fingers touching, coaxing her nipples erect. She opened her eyes to Knox's gaze, soft with affection.

"You are so beautiful," Knox said quietly. "More than I ever imagined."

"So, you've imagined me naked?" A shiver of pleasure ran through her at the thought.

Knox blushed, but chuckled. "Every night, lying here with my hand between my legs, reliving that kiss and trying not to shatter the overhead light."

Salem looked up. "What on earth, Knox?"

"Chemical illumination encased in plastic, not glass, tubes. It's the same principle as those glow sticks emergency responders use at accident scenes. "

"Clever."

"A necessary modification after the homework you gave me busted three light fixtures and turned my brass bed into a twisted wreck. Didn't know brass could bend that easily."

"That explains why your mattresses are sitting on the floor."

"Yeah. I need to shop for a wood bed frame that doesn't absorb and conduct an electrical charge."

Knox's fingertips had resumed their exploration and Salem stretched like a contented cat. "What else did my student learn?"

Knox's eyes darkened as she snagged Salem's hand and pressed the palm to her lips, then sucked the sensitive nerves inside her wrist. "Well, professor, I did a little extra-credit research on the most sensitive areas of a woman's body."

"Oh." Salem pulled her down for a kiss. "I can't wait for that report."

❖

"That's right, hon. We serve breakfast all day." Gina poured them two cups of coffee.

Salem surveyed the menu. Her night with Knox had healed the worry that cramped her stomach for the past four days, and she was ravenous. "I'll have the big country breakfast and a large glass of orange juice."

"Me, too," Knox said. "But I want milk. And extra bacon and a waffle on the side."

"Oh, that sounds good."

"I'll split it with you. But I want a piece of pecan pie while we wait for our breakfast."

"Make that two."

Gina raised her eyebrow. "Is that all, ladies? Would you like strawberries and whipped cream on that waffle?"

"Butter and syrup's okay for me." Salem had other ideas for whipped cream later.

"All righty then. Try not to gnaw on the table before I get back."

Salem watched Knox stir her coffee and made a mental note. Two creamers and three sugar packets. She wanted to know everything about Knox. She wanted to touch her in all the places she'd never been touched before. As if reading her thoughts, Knox looked up and smiled. A sense of elation flowed around, through Salem like a drug injected into her veins. God, this woman was definitely addicting.

"Well, I figured it would take wild horses to drag you out of the house today after the hours you've been working." June stood next to their table and smiled. "Look who's here, Evan."

"Hey, ladies. Y'all mind if we join you?"

"They may not want company, hon," June said, patting Doc on the arm.

"It's cool, Doc Evan," Salem said, taking the opportunity to slide out of the booth and resettle next to Knox, close enough to satisfy her need to touch her.

Gina set two large slices of pie on the table. "Y'all better order fast. We may not have much left in the kitchen by the time these two dainty appetites are done."

"We're starving," Knox declared, digging into her pie.

"Your father always said exercising horses made you eat like one, Knox. You two been out riding early?"

Knox wolfed down another big bite. "Not today. We just got out of—" She stopped in mid-sentence and flushed a deep red.

The twinkle in June's eyes said they were so busted, and Knox looked like she wanted to crawl under the table, so Salem stepped in to rescue her.

"Why, June, you've restyled your hair. I love it."

June grinned and allowed Salem's redirection. "Are you sure it's not too young-looking for me?"

"Not at all. It takes years off you." Salem nudged Knox, who was glancing impatiently toward the kitchen. "Right?"

"Uh, yeah." She stared at June as though seeing her for the first time. "You look like a model out of a magazine, June. Doc Evan might have some competition once word gets around town."

June laughed and leaned against Doc's shoulder when he scowled at Knox. "Oh, Evan's got nothing to worry about." She was rewarded with an affectionate smile from Doc before he shot Knox a look of triumph.

The three women laughed and Salem realized that this moment, sitting with Knox's energy curling around her and sharing a meal with genuine friends, was one of the happiest she'd experienced since childhood. It felt like family. A different kind of family, but definitely a second chance for each of them—a widow, a widower, and two orphans.

It took Gina three trips to load their table with two lunch specials and everything Knox and Salem had ordered. She refilled their coffee cups and lingered even though a group had just filled a table across the room and was waiting to give their orders.

"What's on your mind, Gina?" Doc never was one to beat around the bush.

"That idiot Lamar was in here for the breakfast rush this morning, spouting off a lot of crap about Knox and yesterday's fire."

Salem stiffened. She hadn't told Knox that she'd seen her riding the outskirts of the downtown area. Had others seen her, too? "What exactly did he say?"

"He was trying to tell people that you had Knox start that fire 'cause you want to run him out of business. Said he had proof y'all are responsible. He also made some nasty remarks about you two being more than friends, if you know what I mean. He was yelling it for everybody to hear."

Shit. Her bubble of happiness burst like a balloon filled too full. Salem wanted to punch Lamar in the mouth. Why couldn't he just leave them alone? She was so tired of being judged and suffering from the prejudices of narrow-minded people. Knox had gone perfectly still, staring down at her plate. The elation she had been radiating disappeared like water down a drain.

"That sorry little son of a bitch." Doc growled. "I'm gonna kick his ass into the next county."

Gina waved her hand dismissively. "Don't need to. I'm betting he's lit out of town already."

"Why would he leave?" Salem figured he'd be meeting with the fire marshal if he really had some kind of proof.

"Well, everybody just let him talk until he started making personal remarks about you two. Then Kevin Pearson stood up, grabbed Lamar by the collar, and pulled him up on his toes."

"Kevin Pearson, who owns the Pawn and Shop?" She'd just updated the policy on his business and gotten him a better deal.

"Yep. That's him. Kevin shook old Lamar like a scrawny cur and says, 'First off, if you had proof, you'd be at the sheriff's office right now, not shooting your mouth off here while we're all trying to enjoy our breakfasts.' Then he says, 'And second, if those two pretty ladies want to spend time with each other, that's their business. If you ask me, I'd a lot rather have them around Oakboro than your lying, skanky ass.'"

"Are we talking about the guy who shaves his head and wears camouflage to church?" Knox asked.

"You go to church?" That surprised Salem.

"No, but that's what Tony said about him."

"Anyway," Gina said loudly to regain the floor, "Kevin says to Lamar, 'Besides, I heard that auditor guy's been asking questions around town about polices you wrote for people while you were working for Franklin. Word is you were skimming and you're about to get caught.' Well, Lamar's eyes 'bout bugged out of his head and he started swearing and taking Salem's daddy's name in vain. So Kevin dragged him to the door and tossed him out."

Salem frowned. "I can fight my own battles, Gina. I've always managed to do fine on my own."

Knox scowled and nodded in agreement.

"Sugar, y'all don't have to fight all alone, but you do have to learn to say thank you when folks offer support."

That was hard to do. People often had ulterior motives. She thought about Kevin, a redneck's redneck. But wasn't she wrong to judge him as a stereotype? Isn't that what people did to her?

"Then I owe Kevin a thank you, but I doubt the rest of the breakfast crowd agreed with him."

"Agreed with him? Girl, every person in the place applauded when he tossed Lamar out. You may not know most of them, but they thought highly of your daddy."

The people across the room waved their menus impatiently at Gina and she waved back. "Gotta go." She tapped Knox on the shoulder. "Y'all are so cute together."

Salem realized her mouth was hanging open and shut it with a snap. She was so confused. She was furious. She glared at June.

"My father deserted me and Mom when he found out I was gay." She felt Knox's hand on her thigh, warm and reassuring. "Is that how everybody in town seems to know about me? Did he ask the whole church to pray for my soul? That has to be it, because I seriously doubt he bragged about me."

June reached across the table for Salem's hand.

"So much like your daddy. So proud and so hardheaded. But don't repeat his mistake by jumping to conclusions and making rash decisions. He paid a dear price for that." June held her hand up to belay Salem's response. "I'll tell you how everybody in town knows about you, but you have to promise to keep quiet until I've finished."

Knox's hand tightened on her thigh and Salem looked up.

"Can't hurt to listen," Knox murmured.

Salem looked skeptical, but she nodded her consent.

"Now, you girls eat while I talk." June waited until they dutifully picked up their forks again. "As I told you before, I worked with your father from the day he moved to that office seventeen years ago. He had little to say about you and your mom for the first several years. Just said he was divorced and that his family wanted nothing to do with him. Far as I could tell, all he did was work and go to church."

"Well, he did go fishing," Doc said. "A hound dog took up at his house that second year he was here, and when he brought it in for shots, he saw my fishing poles. We got to talking and I invited him to go fishing with me and Jeff. It got to be a regular thing."

June patted his hand affectionately. "That must have been what made the difference. I'd been working for your daddy about three years when I first noticed the picture of you and your mom in his office. But I reckon the big Steve Scott blowup was about five years after Franklin moved here."

"I still can't believe that whole thing happened," Doc said.

"Steve had been the band director at Oakboro High School for three years, and he had those kids winning every band award around here. They even went to Atlanta and placed third in the state competition. Anyway, he met his partner, Martin, over in Valdosta and, after about a year, Martin moved here to live with Steve. They didn't flaunt it, but Martin, bless his heart, is hard to miss. It wasn't long before some of the village idiots around here, most from your daddy's church and pretty influential in town, started some noise and got Steve fired."

Gina had wandered over to refill their coffee cups again and lingered to interject her two cents. "It was that snotty Sheila that started it all. She was pissed her kid didn't get picked to go on the state-competition trip."

"Yes, well, when word got around that the school board was scheduled to hear Steve's appeal, your daddy got on the phone and started calling people. Must have been three hundred parents and students who showed up to speak on Steve's behalf. And, after your daddy made the most eloquent speech this county has ever heard, the board voted unanimously to reinstate Steve in his old job. They gave him a raise, too." June consulted her watch. "Oh, dear, I have to get back to the office." She gave Salem's hand one last pat. "I'll get Katie to send over a copy of the minutes of that meeting in case you want to read it sometime."

Salem barely registered their good-byes.

Since the day her father had caught her kissing her first girlfriend, she'd learned to expect bigotry and condemnation from family members, co-workers, strangers, and even people who professed to be her friends. And that was in Atlanta, where people were better educated, better informed, and, supposedly, more enlightened.

She hadn't expected acceptance and true friends in this small Southern enclave where almost everyone was in church on Sunday morning, folks were still careful not to wear white before Easter or after Labor Day, and a vacant building burning downtown was the biggest event of the year.

Chapter Twenty-three

Salem was grateful that Knox seemed comfortable with her silence as they drove to her house to check on Tuck. Her thoughts, her emotions churned over everything June had told her. If her father had spoken up for a gay man here in Oakboro, why had he remained a loud silence in her life?

Tuck, having made use of his newly installed pet door, was lounging on the deck when they pulled around to the back door of Salem's house. He mewed a greeting to Salem, then strolled over to Guardian when Knox lifted him from the Jeep to the ground. Purring, he rubbed his cheek against the big dog's leg, then stood on his hind legs to rub his face against Guardian's.

"Well, Guard, I guess this is a day for finding friends in unexpected places," Knox said. Looking worried, she lifted Salem's hand to brush it against her lips. "Are you okay?"

Salem sighed and cuddled into Knox's offered embrace for a long hug. "I don't really know, but it's time to find out."

She took her box of unopened letters and they settled on the couch. Salem snuggled between Knox's long legs to rest her back against Knox's chest. She felt safe, protected by Knox's energy. She was ready to face this now.

"You shared your demons with me last night. Now I need you to help me with mine today."

"Anything, sweetheart," Knox said, her voice soft in Salem's ear. "What's in the box?"

"Letters my dad wrote to me. Lucille, a woman my dad 'kept company with' after he moved here, gave them to me a couple weeks ago." She fingered the letter on top. Next to her address, written by her father, was her own handwriting. "Return to sender," it said. "I…I haven't read them because I figured they were just full of preaching, and that pissed me off. But now I'm not so sure. I've been wrong about some other things lately. Maybe I was wrong about him, too."

"You want to read them now?" Knox's arms slid around Salem, her hands warm and reassuring against her ribs.

"I think I do."

She carefully opened the first, the letter that the hurt and angry teen had sent back unread seventeen years ago.

Dear Salem,

I miss you and your mother so much. There is so much I want for you, my daughter.

I'm afraid I was too hasty and severe with you. You are young and crushes on your friends are common at your age. Things will change as you mature.

I really wish you would come visit me in Oakboro. It's a wonderful place with good people. You would see that if you would visit, perhaps this summer after school lets out.

I've found a good church family here…

She frowned. If she'd read this letter all those years ago, she probably would have burned it.

Knox's kiss was brief against her neck. "Read the next, sweetheart. June said his views changed after he'd been here a while."

Salem picked up the next one and hesitated. Truth was, she'd started to feel better about her father and was afraid that reading these letters would make her hate him again. She didn't want to do that. She wanted to love him like she did when she was a little girl.

She tore open the envelope.

...I went fishing with my friend, Evan, today and met a young man. His name is Jeff and he lives with another young man, Tony, who works at Evan's veterinarian clinic. That surprised me because Jeff doesn't fit what I've come to expect a gay man to be like. He's a real guy and loves the outdoors.

We talked for a long time about that and he's given me some things to think about...

A flurry of letters that followed related Franklin's theological debates with Jeff. Tears fell as she read the last of six letters her father had mailed and she had returned unopened.

I can never tell you how much I wish I could undo the damage I've caused. I am so sorry.

I know I deserve your anger, but it cuts my heart that you have blocked my phone calls and told your mother I am dead to you.

Yes, your mother and I talk on occasion. You weren't the only person I hurt when I abruptly moved to Oakboro. She has forgiven me, but her trust was too damaged to repair our relationship. Even so, she'll always be the only woman I've ever loved, and you, my daughter, will always be more than I deserve.

The letters after that were simply postmarked, but never sent, just as Lucille had said. The first was dated right after her high-school graduation.

...I watched you today and it made my heart swell, my darling daughter.

I wanted to hold you in my arms and tell you how much I love you, but you were smiling and laughing with your mother and friends, and I didn't want to intrude and ruin your day.

If you ever read these letters, the one thing I want you to remember from them is that I am so proud of you.

Salem pushed the box of letters to the floor and sobbed against Knox's shoulder. She cried for the father she had loved as a child.

She cried for the years lost with him. Mostly she cried because, while his actions tore them apart, she was responsible for their continued estrangement.

Knox's aura, normally sharp and constantly moving, softened and stilled to wrap Salem in a soothing blanket.

When her crying quieted, she returned the scattered letters to the box. The past two weeks of emotional highs and lows left her too raw to read them all now.

She led Knox to the bedroom where they stripped their clothes off to slip under the covers together. She needed to feel Knox's skin on hers, Knox's pulse beating in time with hers. She needed for Knox to touch and heal the damaged pieces of her heart.

❖

Salem woke to a lingering sadness but felt gloriously rested and unfettered. The anger she'd dragged like a heavy chain was gone. She'd arrived in town a bitter refugee and had found friends in Oakboro.

And there was Knox. The warm body she was using as a pillow held a heart so pure and untouched, Salem wanted to cradle it gently, nurture it, shelter it.

She moved her palm over Knox's lean flank, tracing each rib with her fingertips until a firm hand stopped her examination.

"Not a morning person?"

Knox blinked sleepily, but held tight to Salem's wrist. "I am, but—" She squirmed just out of reach when Salem tried to resume her pleasurable exploration.

"You're ticklish." Salem grinned and attempted to free her hand.

"No. I'm not."

"Yes, you are." She was no match for Knox's strength, so she closed her lips around an exposed nipple and sucked hard. When Knox's grip relaxed, Salem jerked free to find her ribs again and laughed at the squealed protest.

"No, stop, Salem—"

Knox laughed and bucked, then Salem's back was against the bed, her own ribs under assault.

But Salem rolled and regained her position on top, laughing as she struggled with the tangled sheets and Knox's frantic efforts to escape the tickling. By the time she realized Knox was suddenly out of her reach, Salem was suspended several feet over the bed.

"Knox! What the—"

The sensation was like floating on something, rather than being weightless. Palms out, Knox was a portrait of concentration, eyes narrowed and lips pressed in a taut line.

Salem laughed. "I didn't even know you could do this. Put me down, you nut."

"No. More. Tickling."

Salem flailed in the air, but she was held fast. She tried a different tack. "I can't kiss you from up here." She licked her lips. "And I really want to kiss you right now." She felt a small wobble, a weakening in the energy field that held her aloft. "Let me down and I'll show you where else I want to put my mouth."

The words were barely past her lips when Salem fell to the bed like a stone and the mattress crashed through the bed's frame. She grabbed onto Knox as the bed tilted and tumbled them to one side. When everything came to a stop, it took a moment for Salem to register exactly what had happened. Then she laughed at Knox's horrified expression. After a few seconds, Knox laughed, too, and they giggled together like schoolgirls until Salem was out of breath and tears were leaking onto her cheeks.

"Oh, my God. I can't believe we broke the bed."

Knox corrected her, still chuckling. "You broke the bed."

"You dropped me."

"You deliberately shattered my concentration."

Salem wiggled her eyebrows suggestively. "You're so easy."

Knox blushed, but smoothed her hand over Salem's butt. "This is all new for me, you know. I want you, want my hands on you, every minute."

Salem melted at the shyness in her voice, the yearning in her eyes. "You can touch me anytime, anywhere, every way you want," she said softly.

"I'd like that," Knox said, "but my other arm is kind of—"

"Oh, God. I must be crushing you." Salem realized Knox's left arm was wedged between the mattress and collapsed bed frame. "Are you okay?" She scrambled up and helped Knox free herself. "Are you hurt?" She kissed a red scrape on Knox's shoulder.

"I'm fine. Just bruised a little." Knox rubbed her elbow. "I can't say the same for the bed."

The mattress lay between the side rails at an odd angle, and the jagged ends of two broken support slats stuck out. Salem eyed the wreckage. The top left corner was held several inches off the floor by something underneath.

"Wonder what's…oh, no. Where's Tuck? Guard!"

But Guardian was lying in the hallway with Tuck curled between his legs, and Salem breathed a sigh of relief. If it wasn't them, what was tilting the mattress? Salem rounded the bed and got down on her hands and knees to look. Something was definitely under there. She switched on the bedside lamp and saw a metal box lodged against the box springs. Ass in the air and chest pressed to the floor, she stretched to get her hand on it.

"Honey, can you come around and lift the mattress? Something's stuck under here."

After a strangled sound behind her, the bulb in the lamp burst and showered her with glass.

"Knox?" Salem pulled her hand back and sat back on her heels to look over her shoulder. "Baby, are you okay?"

Knox swayed, covering her eyes with her hands. "No. I'm not. You're going to kill me. I'm having a stroke."

"What are you talking about?"

"You're naked."

"We're both naked."

"But you were…" Knox used one hand to keep her eyes covered and pointed with the other "…down there, you know… with your, you know…sticking up…" She swayed again. "God, I'm gonna faint."

Salem got to her feet and steered Knox into a chair. "Breathe, baby. You're hyperventilating. Take slow, deep breaths."

Shaking her head, she stepped into the bathroom to wet a washcloth and slip into her robe. She kept forgetting Knox was a twenty-eight-year-old with the sexual experience of an adolescent. She held the cool cloth to Knox's neck and chuckled at her flushed face. "You can open your eyes. I've put my robe on now."

Knox opened only one eye to confirm she was clothed before she opened the other.

"Keep holding this washcloth to your neck. I'll be right back."

She retrieved another robe from her father's closet and helped Knox into it when she stood. "Feeling better?"

Knox averted her eyes and stepped back. "Yeah. Better." But she crossed her arms and tucked her hands tightly away.

"What's wrong?"

Knox shook her head.

"Are you upset with me?"

Another headshake and another step back. She wasn't hiding in her lab or taking off on her horse, but Knox was retreating again, and Salem wasn't going to let her get away with it this time. She wrapped her in a tight hug. Knox was trembling.

"We're not going to play twenty questions, Knox. I'm going to hold on until you tell me what's wrong."

They stood there for a long moment until Knox returned Salem's embrace.

"It's just…when I saw you down there like that…I wanted…I wanted to—"

Salem smiled against the soft flannel covering Knox's chest. "You wanted to jump my bones?"

"I wanted…to do things to you." Knox groaned. "God, I'm such an ass."

Salem cupped Knox's face. "Baby, you are not an ass. I like that you want to do 'things' to me. I hope we'll both be doing lots of things to each other. But we've got plenty of time to explore that. Right now, I need to see what's under the bed. Okay?"

Knox let out a shuddering breath. "Yeah."

Salem gave her a chaste kiss, mindful now that Knox's inexperience was a sexual powder keg. One she would gladly light later. "Lift that mattress for me?"

"Yeah, sure."

Salem sat on the floor cross-legged and set the file-sized metal box on her lap. The catch appeared to be locked when she thumbed it, so she turned it over to see if a key might be taped underneath.

"Maybe it has cash in it," Knox said.

"It doesn't look like a cash box…more like a file container. It probably just holds important papers, like the title to his car or something."

"His lawyer didn't give you all those documents?"

"Well, yeah." Salem turned it right side up and jiggled the catch again. "Can't you just…you know, like you did the car locks?"

Knox chuckled. "I'm not sure I can focus right now. You sorta blew a few of my fuses." She took the box from Salem. "But I am an engineer. Find a paper clip and I'll have it open in two seconds."

"Okay." Salem jumped up and trotted into her father's study. The second drawer she opened held a box of paper clips and a small key. "Hey, here's a key that may fit it," she yelled.

"Bring a paper clip, too, in case it isn't the right one," Knox yelled back.

The key did open the box, which was filled with a ledger, receipts, and several file folders.

A letter on top confessed the cause of the stable fire and Lamar's threats to expose the lie on the insurance claim. The claim would have been paid even if the real cause had been originally listed, but the affidavits falsified to protect Ham could have invalidated the policy and cost Franklin his insurance license.

Salem opened the ledger and studied the figures and writing. She recalled Dan mentioning several of the clients he interviewed about suspicious policies said Franklin had asked the same questions several months before his heart attack.

"This is it, Knox. This is the evidence we need to nail Lamar. It looks like my father was building his own case against him before he got sick."

Knox looked at her. "You don't think Lamar—"

"No. My dad had progressive heart disease. There was nothing suspicious about his death."

"Good. That's good. Because if Lamar tried to hurt you—"

Salem could feel Knox's energy change, snapping around them. "I don't think Lamar's dangerous." She stroked Knox's forearm and rested her shoulder against Knox's. She was surprised, but pleased, at the fierceness in Knox's eyes. "Stupid, but not dangerous."

"What are you going to do with this?"

"I should fax all of it to Dan." Salem returned the files to the box and closed it. She looked at Knox. "Your father's gone, my father's gone. You don't have to protect your brother any longer." She took Knox's hand in hers. "But the insurance underwriter could decide to sue your father's estate for the money they paid out."

"Money isn't an issue. I could afford to build that barn ten times over at today's prices. If they want repayment, they won't have to sue. I'll willingly reimburse them. It's the right thing to do, Salem."

Salem gave her hand a squeeze. "It's settled then. You okay with cereal for breakfast or do you want to go to the diner?"

"We're getting dressed and going to your office now?"

Salem laughed. Knox's pout made her look like a kid who'd just learned she wouldn't have ice cream for dessert. She stood and dropped her robe to the floor. "Only after I introduce you to the joys of showering together. Then we can have a quick breakfast of Captain Crunch and go to my office."

"Thank God. I was afraid you'd make me eat granola or something healthy." Knox stood and dropped her robe as well. "Besides, I was thinking of putting something else in my mouth."

"I so love a quick student."

Chapter Twenty-four

Cradled back to front in the curve of Knox's long torso, Salem's feverish body seemed to sizzle under the suddenly icy spray.

"Oh, baby, so good, so good." The sweet invasion of Knox's long fingers and the energy that poured from them filled Salem with almost unbearable pleasure. She reached behind to slide her hand between their slick bodies and her fingers found their mark against Knox's stiff clitoris. Knox pumped against Salem's ass and groaned. The thrusts grew urgent, and Salem's sensitive clit swelled under the rough massage. Her muscles tightened around Knox's fingers as they filled her again and again, until she could no longer breathe and it was too much to hold inside.

"Do it, baby, do it. Make me come," Salem gasped.

The force that was Knox, pure and primal, surged, burned, and Salem cried out at the exquisite orgasm roiling through her body. Her screams and Knox's shout echoed off the shower walls that vibrated with the power of their coupling.

Riding out the waves of her climax, she clenched her thighs together, both to still Knox's hand and hold her inside as long as possible. Knox's clit jumped and twitched against her fingers for another long moment.

Thankful that Knox's legs, muscled and strong from years of riding horses, had held them upright, Salem took a long breath and turned in Knox's arms. She couldn't resist rubbing her cheek against

Knox's hard nipple and smiled when she felt her shudder. "Even if you hadn't asked me to keep your gift a secret, I still wouldn't tell anyone."

Knox's lips were soft on hers. "You wouldn't?"

"I don't want other women to find out how criminally good you are at making love."

Knox's smile was shy. "I was a little worried about that. I mean, um, you know, how I stacked up against other women you've been with."

"Are you kidding? If it ever got out how incredibly super-califragilistic you are, I'd have to become a serial killer to keep the women away from you."

When Knox laughed, her aura blossomed and tingled through every cell of Salem's body.

"It's not just me, you know." Knox's eyes were silver and sharp with certainty. "It's both of us, together. I felt it the first time I met you." She smoothed her hands over Knox's ass and realized she was ready, wanted Knox again.

"That's a very interesting theory, Dr. Bolander." She tugged Knox toward the bedroom. "But I think it needs more research."

❖

Salem sat with her shoulder pressed against Knox's as they refueled on sugary cereal, eating from the same large bowl. She couldn't put a name to it, but she sensed this bonding with Knox was very different from anything she'd experienced. She felt compelled to touch her, be with her every second. Knox made her feel strong and vital, soft and serene. She worried that Knox could create this same euphoria in any number of women. Salem had let the horse out of the barn without knowing if it would follow her or run after the herd.

"What are you worrying over?"

Salem started to lie, just a little lie that people tell to keep their thoughts secret. But she realized Knox could read her emotions, just as she could feel Knox's. So, she told the truth. "Silly, stupid things."

She set the dregs of their breakfast on the floor so the animals could finish. Guardian watched as Tuck half crawled into the bowl to lap at the milk, then he gingerly licked up his share from the other side. "Let's go fax these papers to Dan, then head out to your place. It's a beautiful day, perfect for a long horseback ride. I can pack a snack for us to eat down by the river."

Knox accepted her change of subject with a brief kiss. "That sounds great. We'll have to come back to town for dinner, though. I've got nothing but wilted lettuce and a can of soup at my house."

"Then let's leave Guard here with Tuck. It'll give them a chance to get to know each other."

Salem retrieved Franklin's box of evidence, leaving Knox to settle Guardian in the living room with his bed and chew bone.

"All set?" Salem asked.

"Yep."

They were at the back door when Salem stopped. "Oh, I need my sunglasses. I think they're in the bedroom. You go ahead. I'll only be a second."

She jogged to the bedroom, found her sunglasses on the dresser, and trotted back to the kitchen. But when she swung the door open, Knox was sprawled, face-first, on the deck.

"Knox! Oh, my God." She fell to her knees and brushed the dark hair back from Knox's face. Her eyes were closed and Salem realized the air around them seemed silent, empty of the current she associated with Knox.

Lamar stepped out from behind her and held up a pistol. "The freak is taking a little nap, courtesy of Smith & Wesson." He bared his teeth in a cruel grin. "Just a little tap on the head and superwoman isn't so super anymore."

Salem felt along Knox's neck, finding her pulse strong and steady. She jumped to her feet, hands balled into fists. "I'm going to beat the shit out of you, you pathetic little worm—"

"Uh-uh-uh." Lamar waved the gun at her. "You might want to rethink that, bitch."

Salem started toward him. "You don't have the balls to shoot me."

"Shoot you?" He swung the gun toward Knox's still body. "I was thinking I'd pump a few bullets into her." He cocked the hammer on his thirty-eight revolver.

Salem instinctively stepped between Lamar and Knox. This guy was crazy. She needed time to think.

"What do you want from us, Lamar?"

"I want both of you queers to pay for messing up my life. That freak made me a laughingstock when we were kids, and now you showed up, stole my business right out from under me, and put the feds on my tail."

"If something happens to us, you'll be the first person the police suspect."

"That's where you're wrong. I've got it all planned out, and finding the firebug here with you is just gonna make things easier." He stepped around Salem and held the gun a few feet from Knox's head. "Now make yourself useful and drag the freak back into the house before I just shoot you both right here."

Salem hesitated. If they went inside, would Guardian hear them? Crap. He was deaf. Besides, just because he was a German shepherd, he wasn't necessarily trained to protect. Would Lamar be less likely to shoot them outside where the neighbors might see or hear? Her neighbors on both sides would be at work this time of day. Did Lamar know that?

Knox groaned and Lamar kicked her in the ribs. "Hurry up, bitch, or I'll have to shoot the freak now before she wakes up."

She flung herself across Knox's body to shield her. "Okay, okay. Don't hurt her." Salem carefully rolled her onto her back and lifted Knox's shoulders to lock her arms around her chest. Knox's head lolled against Salem as she slowly stood and walked backward inside the house.

Once inside, Lamar pulled a coil of thick twine from his pocket. "Lay the freak on the floor and you sit in that chair." The twine was rough and bit into Salem's ankles and wrists where he tied her to the chair.

She frantically looked around the kitchen, searching for an idea, a weapon that would get them out of this mess. Her fear rose, bitter in her mouth, with each minute Knox remained unconscious. How hard had he hit her? Tears burned her eyes. She had to get free. She had to help Knox.

Lamar jerked Knox onto her stomach and tied her hands behind her back. He didn't notice Tuck crouched in the doorway to the living room, eyes fixed on the twitching twine as Lamar squatted to wrap it around Knox's ankles. When the kitten pounced, Lamar fell on his butt. "Son of a bitch." He grabbed Tuck and threw him against the wall. The kitten landed on his feet and fled to the living room. Lamar forgot about tying Knox's legs and laid his gun on the table. He began to rummage through the kitchen drawers.

If only she could get her hands on that gun. She struggled against her bindings, but the twine only cut deeper, sharper into her flesh. Knox's eyelids fluttered and Salem knew she needed to distract Lamar until Knox was fully awake.

"You won't get away with this, you bastard."

His laugh was harsh. "That's where you're wrong. I've got a tidy stash built up from the money I've been skimming from your clueless old man. I'll be long gone before that auditor gets back, and the cops won't waste time chasing me across the country for a simple insurance-fraud crime."

"They'll hunt you down for murder if you hurt us."

He threw his head back and chortled. "Wrong again. The whole town knows the freak set fire to her daddy's stable when she was a kid. I made sure yesterday's fire looked like arson so I can pin it on her."

Lamar's eyes were overbright and sweat rolled down his jaw. Was he high on drugs? Which was more dangerous, a crackhead or an insane person? Did it really matter?

"Why would anyone believe Knox set that fire?" She kept her voice calm, refusing to let him see her fear.

"Everybody in the diner saw the bitch lose her cool with me the other day." He yanked another drawer open and smiled when he found what he was searching for. "She burned my building down to get back at me."

"That's a pretty big leap, don't you think? The cops aren't going to fall for that without some kind of evidence."

He set a small candle on the table and put his face close to Salem's. He stank of sweat and stale cigarettes.

"Now here's the genius part. I saw her on that fancy horse, watching the fire from the edge of town. So I followed 'em, and when that horse took a crap, I collected a bag full and dumped it in the alley behind the old store. Even that Barney of a sheriff knows horse shit when he steps in it."

Tuck reappeared in the darkened doorway. This time, Guardian stood behind him, watching them. But Lamar, his back to the animals, was too deep into his story to notice. He stepped back and lit the candle with matches from his pocket.

"You see, the firebug just can't help herself. So, when you two queers have a lovers' quarrel, she goes crazy, lights this candle, turns on the gas stove over there, and blows both of you and the house into a million pieces." He grinned at her. "Told you I was a genius."

Knox's eyes were open now, but unfocused. She groaned and Lamar snatched up his gun from the table.

"Don't make me shoot you, freak. I don't want them finding a bullet in your charred body." He held the gun awkwardly while he bent to finish tying Knox's feet. A length of twine dangled from his pants' pocket and Tuck sprang for it, digging his claws deep into Lamar's leg.

Lamar cursed and swatted at the kitten. Guardian lunged, sinking his teeth into the wrist of Lamar's gun hand. Lamar howled and the revolver fired, sending a bullet into the floor near Knox's head.

"Knox!" Salem screamed, helpless to protect her.

Knox, awake now, rolled away and scrambled to sit against the wall. Bullets fired wildly around the room as Lamar struggled to get free of the dog. Several pumped into the kitchen's vinyl flooring and another whizzed past Salem. She ducked, then ducked again as a cast-iron frying pan flew across the room and banged into Lamar's head, dropping him with a thump.

The room went quiet and Knox sagged against the wall, her eyes closed. Guardian went to her, whining and licking her face.

"Knox, baby, are you all right?"

"Head hurts. That frying pan was heavy." She kicked the twine Lamar had never finished tying away from her feet and pushed against the wall to stand. She swayed, her face pale, eyes filled with worry. "He didn't hurt you, did he?"

"No, I'm fine." Fine now that Knox was conscious and talking.

Knox stumbled over to her and bent down awkwardly, her hands still tied behind her back, to rub her cheek against Salem's. Her lips were soft against Salem's neck. "I'm afraid to think what I'd do if he *had* hurt you."

Salem turned her head, her lips finding Knox's. "I was so scared for you. You took so long to wake up." She was desperate to wrap her arms around Knox, to reassure herself that Knox was truly okay. "Can you use that wonderful brain of yours to untie us?"

"How about I just find a knife to cut us loose? It'll be a lot quicker."

Chapter Twenty-five

Knox breathed deeply, sucking in the night air that had grown blissfully cool. They still had a number of hot days left before winter, but tonight held a hint of autumn. The cool eased the throbbing of her head, and the chorus of crickets and their horses cropping grass nearby was a soothing symphony.

The sheriff's office had been bedlam.

After she freed them, Knox had bound Lamar with his own twine while Salem called the police. Nearly the entire force of twenty deputies crowded into the small house, so Sheriff Thurman Whitaker ordered everyone downtown to sort out who did what.

News traveled fast in Oakboro. June and Doc were already at the jail to fuss over them when they arrived, and Lucille, burdened with being Lamar's mother, was a few minutes behind them. She brought along her pastor, for support, and the pastor's wife, who was a local defense attorney.

Dr. John Whitaker, the sheriff's brother, was summoned to examine both Knox's and Lamar's head injuries. He told Knox to take it easy for the next twenty-four to forty-eight hours and cautioned Salem to keep a close eye on her. He declared Lamar too stupid and thickheaded to be hurt.

Then the fire chief came to interrogate Lamar, and a handful of his firefighters showed up because they heard the chief was called in. The party was complete when the mayor and the full city council joined the ruckus.

Knox was normally a solitary person, so the press of people and multitude of questions was too much for her. She struggled to hold down her nauseating claustrophobia and the overwhelming desire to jump up and run for someplace quiet.

Salem seemed to sense this and persuaded the sheriff to take their official statements tomorrow when Knox was feeling better.

And they escaped.

Still, Knox couldn't settle. The past two days had been a gauntlet of gut-wrenching emotion. Stark fear, burning anger, fierce protectiveness, and consuming love, so sweetly painful she couldn't yet speak of it. The feelings warred within her like whitecaps on an angry ocean, fighting to be the wave that pitched the boat over.

So Knox turned to what grounded her most. Riding had always been her path to peace and clarity.

They saddled Bastille and Legacy and wound through the maze of trails for hours until they finally stopped beside the pond where the tall, ancient pine still stood sentry. Now, lying on the blanket with Salem cuddled against her side, Knox finally relaxed. The familiar ride and the cadence of the horses' hoofbeats had again untangled her jumbled emotions.

"Remember the first time we came here?" she said softly. She felt Salem smile against her shoulder.

"You mean when I tried to kiss you and you freaked out?"

Knox chuckled. "Yeah. You were blowing every synapse in my brain."

"You were like a skittish horse, dancing away every time I approached you, but following every time I turned my back."

"I was afraid for you to touch me." Knox swallowed to ease the lump that was forming in her throat. "I was scared that if you found out who, what I was, you'd go away like all the others."

Salem rose on her elbow, her eyes soft with affection, her hand warm against Knox's cheek. "You aren't still afraid, are you?"

"More than ever." The whispered admission escaped before Knox could think to hold it back.

"Why, baby? Why are you still afraid?"

Salem's aura surged, entwined with hers, and Knox closed her eyes to let it steady her. She knew they couldn't have any more secrets between them. She opened her eyes and held Salem's gaze.

"Because I've fallen in love with you. I've never been in love before and it scares me to death."

Salem's eyes, her smile lit up to rival the full moon illuminating the paths that led them to this clearing, this moment. She brushed her lips against Knox's, a caress so reverent and sweet Knox wanted to cry.

"Don't be scared, sweetheart. I feel the same way. What's happening between us is so different, so much deeper, I'm sure this is the first time I've fallen truly, madly in love, too."

The last door now opened wide, Knox laid claim to this woman who had gently touched her and unleashed everything her fear had held inside.

And, as their kiss deepened and their passion unfurled, the old pine fanned its long needles and the surrounding oaks danced.

About the Author

Jackson Leigh grew up barefoot and happy, swimming in farm ponds and riding rude ponies in rural south Georgia.

Her love of reading was nurtured early on by her grandmother, who patiently taught her to work *The New York Times* crossword puzzles in the daily paper, and by her mother, who stretched the thin family budget to bring home grocery store copies of Trixie Belden mysteries and Bobbsey Twins adventures that Jackson would sit up all night reading.

Her passion for writing led her quite accidentally to a career in journalism and North Carolina where she now feeds nightly off the adrenaline rush of breaking news and close deadlines. She is a hopeless romantic with a deep-seated love for anything equine.

Friend her at facebook.com/d.jackson.leigh, follow her on twitter @djacksonleigh, or visit her Web site at www.djacksonleigh.com.

Books Available from Bold Strokes Books

Slingshot by Carsen Taite. Bounty hunter Luca Bennett takes on a seemingly simple job for defense attorney Ronnie Moreno, but the job quickly turns complicated and dangerous, as does her attraction to the elusive Ronnie Moreno. (978-1-60282-666-3)

Touch Me Gently by D. Jackson Leigh. Secrets have always meant heartbreak and banishment to Salem Lacey until she meets the beautiful and mysterious Knox Bolander and learns some secrets are necessary. (978-1-60282-667-0)

Missing by P.J. Trebelhorn. FBI agent Olivia Andrews knows exactly what she wants out of life, but then she's forced to rethink everything when she meets fellow agent Sophie Kane while investigating a child abduction. (978-1-60282-668-7)

Sweat: Gay Jock Erotica edited by Todd Gregory. Sizzling tales of smoking-hot sex with the athletic studs everyone fantasizes about. (978-1-60282-669-4)

The Marrying Kind by Ken O'Neill. Just when successful wedding planner Adam More decides to protest inequality by quitting the business and boycotting marriage entirely, his only sibling announces her engagement. (978-1-60282-670-0)

Dark Wings Descending by Lesley Davis. What if the demons you face in life are real? Chicago detective Rafe Douglas is about to find out. (978-1-60282-660-1)

sunfall by Nell Stark and Trinity Tam. The final installment of the everafter series. Valentine Darrow and Alexa Newland work to rebuild their relationship even as they find themselves at the heart of the struggle that will determine a new world order for vampires and wereshifters. (978-1-60282-661-8)

Mission of Desire by Terri Richards. Nicole Kennedy finds herself in Africa at the center of an international conspiracy and being rescued by beautiful but arrogant government agent Kira Anthony, but is Kira someone Nicole can trust or is she blinded by desire? (978-1-60282-662-5)

Boys of Summer edited by Steve Berman. Stories of young love and adventure, when the sky's ceiling is a bright blue marvel, when another boy's laughter at the beach can distract from dull summer jobs. (978-1-60282-663-2)

The Locket and the Flintlock by Rebecca S. Buck. When Regency gentlewoman Lucia Foxe is robbed on the highway, will the masked outlaw who stole Lucia's precious locket also claim her heart? (978-1-60282-664-9)

Calendar Boys by Zachary Logan. A man a month will keep you excited year round. (978-1-60282-665-6)

Burgundy Betrayal by Sheri Lewis Wohl. Park Ranger Kara Lynch has no idea she's a witch until dead bodies begin to pile up in her park, forcing her to turn to beautiful and sexy shape-shifter Camille Black Wolf for help in stopping a rogue werewolf. (978-1-60282-654-0)

LoveLife by Rachel Spangler. When Joey Lang unintentionally becomes a client of life coach Elaine Raitt, the relationship becomes complicated as they develop feelings that make them question their purpose in love and life. (978-1-60282-655-7)

The Fling by Rebekah Weatherspoon. When the ultimate fantasy of a one-night stand with her trainer, Oksana Gorinkov, suddenly turns into more, reality show producer Annie Collins opens her life to a new type of love she's never imagined. (978-1-60282-656-4)

Ill Will by J.M. Redmann. New Orleans PI Micky Knight must untangle a twisted web of healthcare fraud that leads to murder—and puts those closest to her most at risk. (978-1-60282-657-1)

Buccaneer Island by J.P. Beausejour. In the rough world of Caribbean piracy, a man is what he makes of himself—or what a stronger man makes of him. (978-1-60282-658-8)

Twelve O'Clock Tales by Felice Picano. The fourth collection of short fiction by legendary novelist and memoirist Felice Picano. Thirteen dark tales that will thrill and disturb, discomfort and titillate, enthrall and leave you wondering. (978-1-60282-659-5)

Words to Die By by William Holden. Sixteen answers to the question: What causes a mind to curdle? (978-1-60282-653-3)

Tyger, Tyger, Burning Bright by Justine Saracen. Love does not conquer all, but when all of Europe is on fire, it's better than going to hell alone. (978-1-60282-652-6)

Night Hunt by L.L. Raand. When dormant powers ignite, the wolf Were pack is thrown into violent upheaval, and Sylvan's pregnant mate is at the center of the turmoil. A Midnight Hunters novel. (978-1-60282-647-2)